With Quill and Ink

A Darcy and Elizabeth Variation

Leenie Brown

Leenie B Books

ISBNs: 978-1-990607-02-8 (ebook); 978-1-990607-03-5 (paperback); 978-1-990607-04-2 (large print)

www.leeniebbooks.com

www.leeniebrown.com

Chapter 1

AUGUST 22, 1811

"What do you think of it?" Fitzwilliam Darcy spared only a cursory glance for his good friend Charles Bingley as the man entered his study.

Bingley had been to visit an estate which had just come into Darcy's possession, one which was close to town and, in Darcy's mind, one which was just the right size for Bingley. Netherfield was neither so large that its upkeep and maintenance would tax his friend's coffers overly much, nor was it so small that it would not give Bingley and his sisters some status.

Bingley's marriageable status, and that of his sisters, would only benefit from the acquisition of an estate. Darcy had always been eager to help his friend improve wherever he wished to improve, and now, as they were both of that age where finding a wife was gaining some urgency, though admittedly more so for himself than Bingley, Darcy was hopeful that his inheritance could benefit his friend.

"Is it as I remember it?" He had always thought Netherfield was a jewel of an estate. The previous owner, one Mr. Enfield, his uncle's cousin, had taken great pride in keeping the place as pristine as possible.

Bingley lowered himself into one of the chairs in front of Darcy's great mahogany desk and tossed his coat onto the chair next to him. "The estate seems to be in good repair, and I believe it is as you described."

He loosened his cravat a touch and pulled at his waistcoat. A breeze blew through the open window, but the day was still warm. Darcy was working in just shirtsleeves today, and those sleeves were rolled up. He was not at home for anyone but Bingley.

"However," his friend continued, "I cannot say for certain if it will match your memories. When was the last time you were there?"

Darcy shrugged and, discarding his pen to its holder, made himself comfortable in his chair. The correspondence in front of him was not overdue, nor did it hold especially time-sensitive instructions for his steward.

"I suppose it was three years ago now." His sojourns at Netherfield had never been long ones. A few days here, a week or two there. Just enough time to visit his relation without having to entertain or be entertained by the neighbourhood, which was just as Darcy liked it.

"Then, I would say little has changed. And as I said, it all appeared to be in very good repair. However, I am not an expert on estates." Bingley untied his cravat, and the piece of material joined his coat on the chair.

"I know. You have told me." Over and over and over. Bingley needed to move past his insecurities about that. Owning an estate was not all that different from owning any other business – not that Darcy was going to say such a thing to his peers. He might say it to Bingley and to his relations, but not his peers for they most certainly did not want to think they had anything in common with a tradesman.

"I did not send you to view the place as an expert. I wanted you to see it before I did so that you could judge for yourself if it is a place you would consider buying without my influence." He leveled a serious look at his friend. "What did *you* think of it?"

"I saw nothing to fault."

"Did you see anything to praise?"

"There was a pretty young lady walking in the lane at the adjoining estate when I rode past."

Darcy shook his head. Of course, Bingley would find a lady to admire. They seemed to materialize out of thin air when Bingley was around. It was as if his charm had some sort of magnetic pull. He would have his pick of ladies to marry once he had an estate to add to his charm and wealth.

If only charm were something someone could purchase, then, Darcy might find himself not dreading the challenge of sifting through the insipid ladies that congregated at the soirees during the season. However, charm was not something that could be purchased. Nor was it something Darcy possessed in great quantities. He struggled to participate in meaningless chatter, and he found it nearly impossible and excessively painful to feign interest in things that did not interest him. What he needed to find was a lady who was both interesting and stirred his heart. But where was such a lady to be found?

He chuckled mentally. Maybe she was in the lane near Netherfield. He only needed to take Bingley with him to draw her out. But that was neither here nor there at the moment, for presently, what mattered was Netherfield itself and Bingley's fondness for it and not the neighbours – pretty or otherwise.

"Is there anything about Netherfield itself that you found to your liking?" Darcy asked.

Bingley nodded and grinned. "There is a fabulous ballroom."

"You are purposefully trying to torment me, are you not?"

"Am I succeeding?"

"Yes." Even if Bingley were not succeeding, Darcy would have said he was to avoid any further teasing. They had been friends for far too long for Darcy to respond any other way.

"Well, then, since I have accomplished that bit of fun," Bingley said, "I will tell you that I enjoyed the gardens and the public rooms of the house. The bedchambers are of a fine size, and the furnishings are appropriate. However, the décor feels a bit tired. A little last century." He leaned back in his chair. "The staff that remains seems friendly and capable."

"And what are your thoughts on owning such a pleasing estate?"

Bingley grimaced. "I am not certain."

Bingley was often not certain. It was one of his less-endearing traits as far as Darcy was concerned. To Darcy, even Bingley's teasing nature was more ingratiating than his indecisiveness because Darcy was not one to waffle when it came to making decisions – well, most decisions. There were a few that caused him to pause, especially since discovering his sister's near calamity in Ramsgate last month.

"Therefore, I think it would be wise for me to take it on lease for a year."

Darcy's eyebrows rose. For being a hesitant fellow, such a commitment was rather decisive for Bingley. "You must truly like it then."

"I do, and I honestly cannot see why you would want to part with it."

"I have enough property. It was generous of Mr. Enfield to name me as his heir, but what do I want with another estate to manage. They are not inexpensive places to maintain." Not that he could not afford to see to its management. He was just not certain it made sense for him to have another piece of land and a home he would only sporadically visit when his friend needed an estate.

"Are you trying to talk me out of taking Netherfield?"

Darcy chuckled. "No. I am simply attempting to help you see the blemishes and not just the beauty. The life of a country gentleman can look far more appealing than it actually is when one gets down to the daily operations."

"How long have I been your friend?" Bingley asked and then did not wait for a reply before answering his own question. "I would say it has been long enough for me to understand the frustrations of a landowner. You are not the sort of gentleman to keep your displeasure to yourself when it is just you and I together." He held up a hand when Darcy opened his mouth to protest. "I count that as a privilege. You must know that. You must also know that I have sat at my father's side through many uncomfortable meetings regarding improvements to mills and the hiring and discharging of employees and suppliers. I have seen many blemishes in life. I just choose not to dwell on them as you do."

"I suppose I am more prone to see the problems," Darcy admitted. It was a point that could not in good conscience be refuted without perjury.

"No truer words have ever been spoken," Bingley agreed with a laugh. "I would like to be settled into Netherfield before Michaelmas. Would that be acceptable to you?"

Bingley must truly be enamoured with the estate if he already had a plan for taking up residence in place.

"As long as the papers can be created in time," Darcy replied, "I see no reason why you could not be settled into Netherfield by then. I will just contact my solicitor –"

"You do not understand," Bingley interrupted.

Darcy's brow furrowed. "What do I not understand? You wish to lease Netherfield. I am happy to allow it. There are papers that must be put in place even for friends when a business arrangement is struck – something of which I know you are aware and would not refute as necessary. What have I neglected?"

Bingley shifted in his seat, and his gaze dropped to the top of Darcy's desk. "I am not an expert on estates."

"Yes, I know, but there is only one way to gain experience."

Bingley shook his head. "No, there is your way, and there is mine."

"Yours?" Darcy asked cautiously.

"Do you know how I learned to tie my shoes?"

"The same way as anyone else. You were instructed." Darcy waved to the books behind him. "These are full of instruction. About estates."

Again, Bingley shook his head. "They are not filled with the sort of instruction with which I do best." He leaned forward. "Do you remember when we were first learning how to play billiards so that we could beat your cousin?"

Darcy chuckled. He and Bingley had spent a few long evenings in gaming hells attempting to find just the perfect person to teach them how to finally defeat Richard. "I do."

"If you remember, you needed only to be told what the best practices were. You could see the angles and schemes in your mind. I was not so fortunate."

Darcy's brow furrowed. That was not how he remembered it. "You grasped the ideas faster than I did." Much faster.

"That is only because they were accompanied by a demonstration and an opportunity for me to attempt them with guidance."

Darcy heaved a deep sigh as understanding dawned on him. "You want me to show you what to do."

Bingley nodded. "I cannot afford to get this wrong. The future of many generations rests upon my shoulders. And I am not speaking just about the ones to follow me. I am also talking about the toil of my father, grandfather, and great-grandfather who worked so I could have this chance to move the Bingley family forward."

"Have you not seen me at work here and at Pemberley?" Darcy remembered many hours of

Bingley sitting in that very chair, or a similar one at Pemberley, and interrupting his work with conversation. Bingley had also accompanied him on several outings around Pemberley to check on work and even lend a hand with some of it. There was no way he did not know at least some of what a landowner did.

"I have, but," Bingley's voice turned pleading, "I have not had the opportunity to put what I have seen into practice, and I might need a hand to turn my cue just enough to make my success more sure." He slouched down in his chair as if someone were pushing down on his shoulders and crumpling him at the waist. "I need you to guide me. I am a quick study, Darcy, but I truly need you. This is too important to not get it right from the start. Will you, please, come to Netherfield with me?"

Darcy's cheeks puffed out and then slowly flattened as he released the air from them. He knew the weight of doing right by a legacy entrusted to him. "By Michaelmas, you say?"

"Before. I want to be settled in by Michaelmas."

Darcy looked past Bingley to the door of his study. "How can I leave my sister? You know she is not well and is just getting settled with Mrs. Annesley."

He and his sister had returned to London only three and a half weeks ago, and Mrs. Annesley had only been with them for the last two of those weeks. His sister's heart was still grieving from the deception that had seen her almost lost to him, and he was reluctant to leave her even for a short time, and the amount of time needed to help Bingley get settled into his role as master of Netherfield would not be small.

Bingley held Darcy's gaze. After a silent moment, the right side of his lips tipped into a half-smile. "I suppose I could wait until spring to take on Netherfield, but I do not see how that will help you. You will still need to visit and see that things are as you wish." He shrugged. "I am sure the expense of time and money to see an estate, which is new to you, through the winter would not be a great difficulty for someone, like you, who is so familiar with the running of estates."

Darcy's eyes narrowed. "Do you know that the majority of the people in this world who have met you think of you as all that is pleasant?"

Bingley nodded and grinned broadly. "And I am."

"No. No, you are not. You, my friend, are shrewd, conniving even."

"You do know that I sat at my father's side through many uncomfortable meetings, do you not? I believe I just reminded you of that fact not long ago."

Darcy shook his head. A Bingley bent on achieving his goal was not easily thwarted. It stood in stark contrast to his natural uncertainty about so many things. Decisions were not easily made, but once the decision had been decided upon, the man became nearly immovable.

Darcy knew that he could just refuse, and Bingley would not press it further for his friend held him in high regard and rarely went against Darcy's wishes on matters of any great importance.

"You could bring Georgiana with you," Bingley suggested.

Darcy frowned as he considered it. "She has lessons which will begin soon. I cannot imagine that there are any dancing masters near Netherfield." The town of Meryton was not dreadful or hopelessly backward. It had a good number of well-kept shops and houses, but it was not London.

"Three weeks," Bingley begged. "Bring your sister with you for three weeks and then, return her to town. Can she not postpone her lessons for that long? By then, she will have been with you long enough for you to know that her heart will continue to heal and that you have not erred so greatly that she will never recover. Of course, I will need *you* to remain longer than three weeks."

"The change of scenery may do her a world of good," Bingley added when Darcy remained silent, save for the drumming of his fingers on his desk. "There may be some young ladies in the area for her to befriend. And you can always bring Richard with you. We could make it a house party of sorts."

One of Darcy's eyebrows arched at that. "I am not attending any sort of house party where your sister Caroline is, and I assume you will be taking her with you, will you not be?"

"I am certain she will not allow me to leave her behind if you are going with me."

Darcy scrubbed his face. "She is handsome, but…" Caroline was not the sort of lady Darcy wished to tie himself to forever. She was a friend and naught else, nor would she ever be anything more.

"I know. You have no plans to make her Mrs. Darcy."

At least one of the Bingleys seemed to have heard him on that. "Very well. Let me see if I can persuade Richard away to the countryside for a few weeks and then, speak to Mrs. Annesley."

Bingley clapped his hands and rubbed them together as if thoroughly satisfied with how his plan was coming together. "And I will send word to Mrs. Nichols to prepare for our arrival." He stood in preparation for leaving, and gathered his discarded coat and cravat, though he made no move to put either back on.

"You are not staying longer?"

"No, I must go tell my sister that we are moving to the country and that the country to which we are moving is not Derbyshire." He paused at the door. "Trust me. I would rather stay here. I have been dreading telling her ever since I arrived at Netherfield and found it to my liking."

Darcy looked at his friend incredulously. "You were planning this whole time to take Netherfield?"

"No, but even the possibility of having to tell Caroline that I was taking Netherfield was enough to make me dread it." His lips tipped up on one side. "Of course, now that I can tell her that you will be there…"

"Remember, I do not plan to marry her. Do not even hint to her that it is a possibility."

Bingley's countenance fell. "And how am I supposed to make this sound like a good idea to her if I cannot tell her that it is a good way to prove herself to you as the mistress of an estate?"

"I do not know, nor do I care. You just must not suggest that there is any hope of my ever considering her beyond her status as your sister and my acquaintance." No accomplishment Caroline Bingley could put on display was going to miraculously earn her Darcy's undying love and devotion as her husband.

"You will have to marry someday, Darcy." There was a teasing tone to Bingley's words.

"As will you," Darcy retorted, "and when that day comes, neither of us will be marrying your sister."

Bingley laughed. "You have made your point. I will try to conjure some other means of placating Caroline."

"I wish you well. Just not well enough to use me as the bait on your hook."

Chapter 2

SEPTEMBER 4, 1811

Elizabeth Bennet shifted her attention from the group assembled in Longbourn's sitting room to the garden. She much preferred being outside to sitting indoors, especially when sitting inside meant listening to her mother, her aunt, and Lady Lucas share interesting bits of information about their neighbours with each other. It was not that she did not find some of the news interesting. Who would not find a story about a rooster chasing Mr. Thompson's grumbly old dog diverting? However, more often than not, the news imparted was the same bits of gossip revisited. There were only so many times she could hear about Mrs. Goulding's niece ordering three new dresses with any amount of affected interest.

"I have heard," Aunt Philips whispered in a way that called the attention of the whole sitting room, including Elizabeth.

The best and newest gossip was always whispered in such a fashion, just in case some newcomer should magically appear at the door to the sitting room without someone in that room knowing a new arrival was imminent.

"The new owner of Netherfield, Mr. Darcy, is an unmarried gentleman with a large," she lifted her brows and emphasized the word large, "estate in the north."

"He is also unmarried and with no prospects, according to what I have heard," Lady Lucas added. "Not that there are not ladies trying to snare him. Ten thousand a year is quite the prize."

Mrs. Bennet clutched the knot of her fichu. "Ten thousand a year?"

Elizabeth saw Jane scoot to the edge of her chair. She was probably preparing to get Mama's salts. Such a sum attached to an unmarried gentleman, who was to be their neighbour, was swoon-worthy in Mrs. Bennet's world.

"At least ten thousand," Lady Lucas replied.

"And he is arriving with a friend who will be leasing the house and park with a thought towards purchasing," Aunt Philips said with a smile and a waggle of her eyebrows for Elizabeth. "Of course, Mr. Darcy's rich, *unmarried* friend cannot buy all of Netherfield since part of it belongs to your daughter. How clever of you, Lizzy, to ingratiate yourself with old Mr. Enfield. There is no way for the gentlemen to arrive and do business without meeting you and your sisters." She looked puffed up enough to burst with delight.

Elizabeth Bennet sighed. "I did not ingratiate myself to Mr. Enfield to have the garden given to me." She had just been neighbourly, admired his garden, and had been allowed to make use of it whenever she wanted. In return, he had named it Elizabeth's Garden and left it to her in his will.

"Of course, you did not," Lydia, Elizabeth's youngest sister, said in a mocking tone.

"I did not! Who parcels out their estate and gives a portion of the park to the lady who lives next door?" Elizabeth shook her head at the strangeness of it all. It had been two months since she had been told about her inheritance, and she still was not certain whether she felt the honor of the gift or the strangeness of it most.

"It does not matter if she did or did not ingratiate herself to earn something on the old man's demise,"

Lady Lucas said before Lydia could do more than make a face at Elizabeth. "The fact remains that you, Fanny, have a daughter who will have to meet the new owner and can put your daughters forward to both him and his friend, who, by the by, has four thousand a year. I will give you that it is substantially less than ten, but it is still a very fine sum."

She leaned forward and lowered her voice while her expression declared that the next bit might be somewhat scandalous. None of the news in Meryton was ever very scandalous, but Lady Lucas did have a flair for the dramatic. "The friend's money is from trade. Not every lady would want such connections, but since your relations are from trade, one of your daughters might do quite well for him."

"What about Charlotte or Maria?" Mary, Elizabeth's next youngest sister, said. "Why does it have to be one of us?"

"Do you not wish to be rich?" Lydia asked in horror.

"Marriage is not all about money," Mary lectured. "Money is important, I will grant you that, but loving money is not to be encouraged. A gentleman's true worth is found in his character and not his coffers."

"The best gentleman will have both good character and a good fortune," Jane, Elizabeth's older sister, inserted to ward off the impending argument that they all knew would follow Mary's lecturing of Lydia. Jane was like that – a true peacemaker – and Lydia was far too self-assured of her own ideas to do anything but argue with Mary when Mary's thoughts disagreed with her own, which was almost always.

"It should be Jane," Elizabeth put forward. "If anyone is going to be able to snare a rich husband and is truly deserving of one with both money and honor, it is Jane. She is far too good and beautiful for us all."

"That she is," Mrs. Bennet said with a lift of her chin and a soft smile for her eldest daughter.

"But what about Charlotte and Maria?" Mary asked again.

Lady Lucas pursed her lips. "Charlotte is going to have a season this year."

"But she could have a husband before the season begins if you put her forward."

"I am content to let fate take its course," Charlotte, the older of the two Lucas daughters, said. "And Maria is far too young to be a wife."

"I am not!" Maria cried. "Why Hettie Gibson was only one year older than me when she married."

"And she has had three children in the space of four years and looks miserable. She is only twenty, and her bloom is completely gone." Charlotte gave her younger sister a glare. "Do you really want that? Or would you rather enjoy a few years of being one of the prettiest girls at the assembly?"

"Not everyone who has a child loses her bloom." Maria's protest was made weakly.

"It happens often," Mrs. Bennet said. "Not everyone can be as fortunate as I was."

Elizabeth had to admit that though her mother was well past the age of being called the prettiest girl at the ball, she was still strikingly good-looking, despite having had five children.

"That is precisely why your daughters might succeed where others have not. They are beautiful," Lady Lucas said. "I am not opposed, of course, to putting Charlotte forward if she wishes it, but as of this morning, she did not."

"Whyever not?" Lydia cried as if such a thought was akin to not wishing to breathe and preferring to die.

"I have my reasons." Charlotte gave Lydia a tight smile.

"It makes no sense to me," Lydia muttered.

It did to Elizabeth. There was a gentleman whom Charlotte had met on a recent trip to London with her father, and she knew that Charlotte hoped to make a match there. Elizabeth's friend was well-suited to life in Meryton, but she dreamed of living in town and making her mark on London's society. Of course, no one else besides Elizabeth and Jane knew of Charlotte's ambitions, and that was how it was going to stay.

"If, by good fortune, one of your eldest daughters were blessed enough to snare Mr. Darcy," Lady Lucas said, "it could prove to be a fabulous boon to both of my daughters as they would have a dear friend in the upper circles."

"Oh! I had not thought of that, but you are right," Mrs. Bennet agreed, while Charlotte gave Elizabeth a pointed look that said she expected Elizabeth to help her in her quest in town.

"It is a good thing that I have two eldest daughters and that there are two wealthy gentlemen settling so close to us," Mrs. Bennet continued. "I only hope to have such good luck when it comes to the other three."

"They will have sisters with wealthy husbands, my dear sister." Aunt Philips's tone was conspiratorial. "They will not need luck."

"Of course, you will first have to get someone to actually marry an odd girl like me," Elizabeth said with a laugh. That was what her mother always said about her and her love of reading and learning things that girls "had no need to know."

Mrs. Bennet gasped and clucked her tongue. "It will not be easy." She tipped her head and looked at Elizabeth. "You are blessed with a good amount of beauty. Not as much as Jane, but adequate. You have only to hold your tongue until Mr. Darcy or his friend is too smitten with you to care that you are impertinent and read too much."

"Yes, one must not let anyone know that women have brains," Mary muttered.

Elizabeth pressed her lips together to keep from laughing. Their mother had obviously not heard the comment for no lecture on what men wanted in wives followed. Of course, what their mother said men wanted in wives was not the same as what Elizabeth's father had told her. He teased his wife that he was certain that there was at least one gentleman in England who wished for something other than a silly wife. His own wife was lacking sense in many areas, but she was not without her cleverness in other areas. It was just that her cleverness did not extend to deep thought and pondering large tomes.

"She will have to do." Aunt Philips's head was tipped the same as Mrs. Bennet's, and the two sisters wore the same expression of mild consternation.

"I will do my best to be polite and welcoming, but I will not hide who I am." Elizabeth had no desire to be tied forever to a gentleman who did not like who she was.

"She will still have to do," Aunt Philips repeated.

Elizabeth had heard enough of this discussion to last her for a few days before she might need a reminder of how unsuitable she was for any gentleman in her mother's and aunt's opinions. "I think I would like to take a walk. Does anyone else wish to join me?"

"Are you going to walk in the garden?" Kitty asked eagerly.

Elizabeth shook her head. "Beyond it."

"Will it be a long walk?" Kitty sounded disappointed by the thought.

"Yes." Long walks usually guaranteed Elizabeth some solitude because if there were not ribbons and lace to be purchased at the end of a long walk, her two youngest sisters found the activity to be pointless.

"Then, I would not like to go with you. However, I will go to the garden."

"And I will go with Kitty," Lydia declared, "And so will Maria."

Poor Maria, and anyone else who was Lydia's friend, often found that their lives and activities were arranged for them by Lydia. Not that Elizabeth was presently too distraught over Lydia's commanding nature. She was just happy to not have her youngest sisters or Maria as walking partners.

"Jane and I will go with you," Charlotte said.

"Of course, we will," Jane agreed. "And Mary, would you like to come with us, too."

"She does," Lydia answered. "Or else she will be by herself."

"Lydia!" Jane scolded. "That is dreadfully unkind."

"She will lecture me."

"Only if you deserve it," Mary retorted, "which you nearly always do."

"Girls!" Mrs. Bennet cried. "None of you will have any husbands if you do not learn to treat each other well. Is that what you want?" She gave Lydia a pointed look.

"No, Mama," Lydia and Kitty said together.

"I could be a governess," Mary replied when her mother turned her eyes towards her.

"Your behaviour and employment reflect on your sisters. I am certain you would not wish to do anything to harm them."

Elizabeth smiled at her mother's particular type of cleverness that could maneuver stubborn children, such as Mary and Lydia, into compliance without the use of punishments.

"Would you?" Mrs. Bennet asked when Mary said nothing.

"No, Mama, I would not, though I am in no hurry to marry."

"Yes, I know. You have told me, but one day, you will meet a gentleman and that will change."

Mary did not look convinced, but, at least, she did not say anything further other than to say she would walk with her older sisters and Charlotte.

"Where shall we walk?" Elizabeth said when they had finally gotten out of the house.

"Towards Netherfield," Charlotte whispered with a glance over her shoulder at their younger sisters who were just entering the side garden. "We might be able to see if there is a reason these wealthy gentlemen are not yet married. Mother assures me that they are both handsome, but you know my mother. She will stretch the truth if it serves her purposes."

That was true. Both Lady Lucas and her husband, Sir William, were prone to exaggeration at times.

"It is three miles to Netherfield," Jane said. "We do not have that much time."

"It is not three miles from here to Elizabeth's Garden if we walk down the lane to the woods. Are you not curious?"

"I am," Mary answered. "What?" She asked when three shocked faces turned her direction. "Just because I said I have no plans to marry for some time does not mean I do not enjoy the search. But do *not* tell Mama I said that." And with that she started down the lane towards the small, wooded area that stood between Longbourn and Netherfield, leaving Elizabeth, Jane, and Charlotte no choice but to follow.

Chapter 3

"Who do you suppose that is?" Caroline Bingley asked from where she stood at the library window, overlooking Netherfield's gardens. She had accompanied her brother as expected, but she had not come happily – or at least not entirely happily. The fact that she had not been able to wiggle her way into Darcy's carriage through claiming a need to spend time with her dear friend, Georgiana, had made her veneer of pleasantness crack and crumble.

It did not matter how close to town Netherfield was. Darcy was not about to subject himself or his sister to the task of entertaining Caroline while she filled his carriage with chatter and smiled coyly whenever she caught his eye.

"Charles, send someone to discover who those people are and remove them from your land," Bingley's other sister, Louisa instructed. Where one Bingley sister went, the other often followed.

"Stand your ground. Allow me to advise."

Darcy's cousin, Richard pushed his way between the Bingley sisters and put a spyglass up to his eye. He had found it on one of the library shelves about an hour ago and had been using it to spy all sorts of things ever since.

For being a well-respected colonel in His Majesty's army, the man often more resembled a child looking for a lark than he did the serious strategist he was known to be. It was not as if he was incapable of being serious and even harsh; it was just that he preferred to play when he could. Darcy supposed that it was the gravity of his profession which drove him to be less serious when he was able to be so.

"Aye, that is a bevy of beauties if I ever did see one."

"Indeed?" Bingley was out of his chair and beside Richard in an instant.

Darcy simply shook his head and remained where he was. "What do you suppose these ladies are doing in your garden?"

"It is not really my garden," Bingley replied before giving a low whistle. The ladies whom he was looking at must truly be pretty to garner such a response. "That one there wearing the green dress looks like the lady I saw in the lane." He turned to Darcy. "And she is not the prettiest."

"Give me that." Percival Hurst, Louisa's husband, snatched the spyglass from Bingley. "If anyone knows what is and what is not to be declared beautiful, it is I."

Darcy wondered if it would not be easier for Hurst to see what was in the garden if he lowered his nose a bit. That man was as arrogant as they came at times. Most of those times happened to occur whenever he thought that an expert's opinion on the quality of an art piece or set of clothes was needed. Hurst was more fashion than function. However, he had married a Bingley sister and reduced the number of Miss Bingleys who flirted with Darcy to one. Therefore, since he had rendered such a noble service, Darcy could not cast him aside completely.

"I say," Hurst continued after he had been instructed by his wife on how to find what he was looking for, "Bingley has the right of it." His tone was one of utter amazement.

"I would not have questioned that," Richard said with a laugh. "Bingley is a charmer and knows a pretty lady when he sees one."

"You make me sound disreputable," Bingley grumbled.

"You could never be that," Georgiana assured him. "Could he, Fitzwilliam?"

"No," Darcy agreed. "Bingley is an honorable fellow. If he was not, I would not keep him as a friend." He patted her hand where it rested on the arm of her chair. He was excessively glad that she had come with him. It did his heart good to see her progress in returning to something of what she was before her heart had been toyed with by his former friend. A *friend* who was not honorable in the least.

"I will remember that," she whispered.

"I have no doubt you will," he replied to her before turning his attention back to the audience that was watching the strangers in the garden. "Shall we go greet our guests, or shall I send someone to bring them to us?"

"They might not come to us," Richard said. "They might escape into the wildwood. I suppose a couple of strong footmen who are fleet of foot could bring us at least two of them."

"Richard!" Georgiana exclaimed with a laugh at his ridiculousness.

How Darcy cherished hearing that laugh again! He stood and held his hand out to his sister. "Come. We will go make sure Richard does not send out an ambush and scare away the neighbours." He looked toward Bingley. "I assume they are neighbors since you did see one in the lane the other day?"

He would like to see this lovely young lady, but he was not about to wrest the spyglass away from his cousin. He would rather meet the neighbours in a more formal fashion.

"I would assume the same," Bingley replied. "I will come with you since I am to learn everything you can teach me, for in a few weeks, I will be the master of this estate for a time."

"You are the master now," Darcy said. "The papers are a mere formality."

"No, no, I choose to wait to be in charge."

"I do not care what you prefer," Darcy retorted. "I am the instructor, and you are the pupil, is that not right?"

"Indeed, it is correct," Caroline inserted with a flutter of lashes for Darcy.

Darcy gave her a tight smile but did not speak further until the person to whom he had addressed the question confirmed that what Darcy had said was correct.

"As your tutor," he then continued, "I say that you are master of Netherfield and responsible for all that happens within and without."

"Which means you must go greet the visitors with Mr. Darcy," Louisa said. "And we will join you. If Hurst says that they are pretty, then it might be a good thing to make their acquaintance. One cannot have too many handsome friends – even in the country."

"One can if one does not want to look less handsome," Richard said with a wink for Caroline who gasped and looked affronted. It was not an unusual look for her to wear when Richard was present. There was no love lost between him and Bingley's sisters.

"It would be best if we all gathered our things and met on the terrace in ten minutes," he continued. "Unless, of course, Bingley's tutor has other instructions."

"No, I think that would be a good plan."

"Right then! Bonnets and hats!" Richard cried as he made a shooing motion toward the door.

"Richard," Darcy called to him before he made his hasty escape from the library. "A trifle less exuberance, please."

Richard chuckled. "I am not certain that is possible. You did hear that there is a bevy of beauties in the garden, did you not?"

"Are you finally going to please your mother and find a wife?" Darcy teased in return.

"One never really knows, does one? Perhaps we will both meet one." He winked and ducked out of the room.

"I would not wager on him finding a wife," Georgiana said. "He seems resolute about staying unattached." She leaned against Darcy's arm as they walked from the library and toward the grand staircase. "I dare say, he is almost as determined as you."

"I will marry when I am ready," he assured her.

"I would like a sister," Georgiana said. "Miss Bingley tries, but…"

"She is not as gentle as you," Darcy finished.

"And has a great deal of difficulty understanding that."

Darcy had been surprised at his sister's reluctance to join him on this trip to Netherfield until she had explained to him that, in essence, she viewed Caroline Bingley in much the same way he did. This confession led quite naturally to his questioning her about why she had never told him about her feelings on the subject before.

Her reply had gutted him, for she had said that she had not wanted to disappoint him by disapproving of his friend's sister. However, she had added, since she already had been a disappointment to him in a most grievous fashion, telling him that she did not prefer Caroline as a close friend did not seem so bad a thing to do.

He had wanted to assure her that she had not disappointed him, but the fact was that she had. She had never, to his knowledge, concealed something of such great importance as having allowed a gentleman to call on her from him before. Wickham wore the greatest share of the blame, but the fact remained that his sister had been secretive. Dangerously so.

"No secrets," he whispered.

It was a promise they had both made to each other after that revelation about only tolerating Miss Bingley due to his relationship with Bingley. It had been secrets that had almost stolen her from him in Ramsgate. He could not abide any more secrecy. Concealment and deception was a treacherous game.

"None," she agreed. "And you?"

"It is the same for me," he assured her. "Unless, of course, it is absolutely necessary to spare you pain. I am, after all, your guardian and not just your brother."

"You will tell me though if you find a lady you like and think you could love, will you not?"

He covered her hand on his arm with his free one. "I will. I would hate to marry someone you could not abide as a sister."

Georgiana was dearer than anything to him. Therefore, any lady who captured his attention and eventually his heart had to first be someone with whom Georgiana felt at ease before he would do more than entertain the idea of marrying her.

"And I shall not marry anyone you cannot tolerate," Georgiana said. "In fact, I promise not to marry or even fall in love until I am twenty."

He chuckled. "You may fall in love earlier than that if it happens once you are out, but you must also know that I am in no rush to be parted from you for any reason."

"You might want to be parted from her so she can get her bonnet." Richard was already returning from his room with his hat and walking stick when they reached the top of the staircase. "Time does not stand still even if you do," he said as he descended the stairs at a gallop.

"Do not greet them without me," Darcy called after him.

"Then be quick," came the reply.

~*~

"Good afternoon," Darcy said ten minutes later as he and the others of his party approached the small section of the garden in which their visitors had first been spied and from which they had not wandered.

Bingley, Richard, and Hurst had not been exaggerating about these ladies being pretty. All four young women possessed varying degrees of handsomeness, and from their manner of dress, appeared to be daughters of gentlemen.

"Good afternoon," the lady in the green dress, and with the most captivating eyes Darcy had ever seen, returned his greeting.

This was the lady Bingley had seen when he had visited Netherfield? It was no wonder he made mention of her when asked if there was anything about the estate that he found to his liking. This woman, with those sparkling eyes and that amused smile, was beguiling. Darcy watched those perfectly pink lips move.

"Are you the new owner of Netherfield?"

Darcy blinked. What sort of spell had she cast over him that he had forgotten his duty in introducing himself? "Yes, I am, but my friend is planning to lease it from me for now."

"Yes, we know," she replied with another of her enchanting smiles.

Were these ladies here to try to snare rich husbands? Darcy's brow furrowed. It would not be the first time he had *happened upon* a lady who had been where she was by design.

"A new arrival in the area is always of interest," his enchantress explained as if she could read his thoughts.

What she said was true in many places, but it still did not put Darcy's mind at ease about whether or not he was prey.

"I am Elizabeth Bennet," she added as if that should mean something to him. Then, she clasped her hands in front of her and waited expectantly. When he did not immediately reply, she prompted him with an "and you are?"

"Forgive me." Embarrassment over having forgotten his duty once again crept up his neck. "I am Fitzwilliam Darcy. This is my sister, Georgiana; my friend, Mr. Charles Bingley; my cousin, Colonel Richard Fitzwilliam; and Bingley's sisters, Miss Caroline Bingley and Mrs. Louisa Hurst, along with her husband, Mr. Percival Hurst."

"It is a pleasure to meet you," Miss Elizabeth said. "Allow me to present to you two of my sisters, Jane –

Miss Bennet – and Mary, as well as our dear friend Miss Charlotte Lucas."

"Two of your sisters?" Bingley inserted.

Of course, Bingley would pick up on that interesting tidbit of information.

"Yes, there are five Miss Bennets in all," Miss Elizabeth replied. "Lydia and Kitty stayed behind at Longbourn with Charlotte's sister, Maria."

"Are there any gentlemen in the area?" Hurst asked in a slightly horrified tone.

Miss Elizabeth's lips twitched while her eyes danced with amusement. She was obviously not the sort of lady to be put out easily. Darcy had to admire that.

"There are none who bear the name Bennet, save for my father. However, Charlotte has three brothers, and there are other families who do not suffer from the dearth of male descendants that ours does."

"Although, to be fair," the one who had been introduced as Miss Lucas interjected, "when you join us for our assembly at Michaelmas you will find that ladies do outnumber gentlemen. Some of it is just due to how things are, and some of it is due to the unsettled state on the continent."

Hertfordshire was not alone in that. There were many places that had seen their population of gentlemen diminished by war.

"What brings you to Mr. Darcy's gardens?" Caroline's tone was a little clipped as her gaze shifted between Darcy and Miss Elizabeth.

He should probably stop staring at Miss Elizabeth, but there was something so familiar about her. He almost felt as if he should know her, which was ridiculous since he had never met her before this very moment. She was not the sort of lady one met and forgot.

"Nothing, in particular, brings us to *my* garden other than the desire to visit it," Miss Elizabeth answered.

That word *my* caught Darcy's attention. "Your garden?"

"Yes, this is Elizabeth's Garden," Miss Lucas said as if it was a fact he should know without being told.

"Did you not know that this is my garden?" Miss Elizabeth asked on the heels of her friend's question.

Darcy shook his head. "You say this is your garden?"

"Yes, Mr. Enfield left it to me."

"He did?" That seemed unlikely. Surely, if a portion of Netherfield's gardens had been bequeathed to another, he would have been told. However, Miss Elizabeth seemed so sure of herself that Darcy was forced to consider that some sort of misunderstanding must be at play.

"Yes. Have you not seen his will?" There was genuine concern in her expression.

"No, I am to meet with Mr. Phillips while I am here to go over the particulars, but he made no mention of there being any part of the estate that was not mine."

"Lizzy!" A gentleman on horseback trotted through the wooded area toward the garden. "Oh, dear," he added when he drew closer. "Mr. Darcy, I presume?" He swung down from his horse.

"Yes, I am Mr. Darcy."

"I had hoped you had not come here today," the gentleman said to Miss Elizabeth. "However, when Kitty said you were gone for a walk, I feared this might be your destination. There are details about Mr. Enfield's will that I need to discuss with Mr. Darcy but was not at liberty to do so until he arrived." He removed his hat and bowed to Darcy. "Mr. Phillips at your service."

This was the solicitor? Darcy eyed him up and down. He appeared to be a reputable sort of fellow, even if he did seem to be less than formal in how he spoke to Miss Elizabeth.

"Miss Elizabeth just informed me that this portion of Netherfield's gardens is hers," Darcy said.

Mr. Phillips worried the brim of his hat. "That would be true, sir. Mr. Enfield left this portion of the gardens to Elizabeth. It was a place that she admired and that he gave her permission to plant and visit as she saw fit."

"Indeed?" Darcy said while others behind him muttered a few *how unusuals*. He had to agree with that sentiment. It was unusual, and it grated to have been caught unaware.

"I assure you that it is true."

"And why was I not informed of this before now?"

"As I wrote to you, your relation, Mr. Enfield, left instructions in his will that you only be told about the inheritance of his estate in general terms until you arrived. I do not know why he chose to do things in this fashion, but my duty is not to question his motives. It is to fulfill his last wishes."

"I see." At least the information had not been neglected. However, that did not make Darcy feel any less awkward about not knowing that this section of the garden was not his. "Enfield was a bit of an eccentric," he added as an explanation more to himself than to anyone else.

"That he was," Mr. Phillips agreed with a smile. "But he was also a good man."

"Thank you. I would agree." Mr. Enfield had been an odd but honorable and amiable gentleman. "Does this affect the lease agreement I requested to be drawn up?" Darcy glanced at Bingley before returning his eyes to Mr. Phillips. He hoped he had not put the idea of taking on Netherfield into Bingley's head only for him to be disappointed.

"A lease will not be an issue. However," the man glanced nervously at Miss Elizabeth, "a sale would be."

"Are you truly planning to sell Netherfield?" Her eyes shifted from Darcy to Mr. Phillips. "My aunt mentioned it was a possibility," she said by way of explanation to the solicitor and then, turned her attention back to Darcy.

"I have considered it," he answered. "I do not need another estate."

Her eyes grew wide at that. Perhaps she did not know exactly how wealthy he was, though that seemed unlikely, given that she knew he was thinking of selling Netherfield.

"Estates are not inexpensive, and Bingley does not yet have one."

She lifted a finger as if thinking and about to speak, but she did not say anything for a moment. "Why is my owning this part of the garden a problem if Mr.

Darcy wishes to sell the estate to Mr. Bingley?" she asked when she finally did speak.

Mr. Phillips grimaced. "Because Netherfield cannot be sold in pieces. It must be sold complete, which means –"

"That I would have to sell my garden with the rest of the estate."

She was not deficient in her ability to put things together quickly. Darcy had to admire that about her also.

"Yes, that is what it means."

"And I would be given a proportional price of the sale?"

She was definitely intelligent.

Mr. Phillips nodded.

"Then, I see no problem if Mr. Bingley proves to be a proper buyer." She smiled at Bingley.

"But there is a further issue." Mr. Phillips swallowed and took a small step away from Miss Elizabeth. "You cannot dispose of your portion until you are married."

"Until I am married?" she cried.

"Yes. Mr. Enfield hoped that this portion of land would help you…" Mr. Phillips took another small step backward. "Find a husband," he added softly.

"Of all the humiliating things!" A hand covered her heart as she closed her eyes and her face pinched as if in pain.

"It was not intended to be a humiliation," Mr. Phillips hurried to assure her. "Mr. Enfield wanted you to find a husband worthy of you, for as he has it written in his will you are 'worthy of only the best of men.'"

"Why did you not tell me this when you met with me?"

Miss Elizabeth's cheeks were flaming, and Darcy felt sorry for how she was discovering this information. His shock at discovering he did not own all of Netherfield was nothing compared to what was becoming her mortification.

"Did you truly want me to tell you this in front of your mother?"

Miss Elizabeth shook her head.

"I had hoped to discuss Mr. Darcy's plans for the estate before I told you about this. It was my hope that he would keep Netherfield, and you... I apologize, Lizzy. I should have told this to you and your father first." He stepped towards her and took her hands. "I thought I was doing what was best. Can you forgive me?"

The corners of her mouth tipped up the tiniest bit as she nodded her head. Her eyes glistened as if her emotions were about to leak out of them.

"May I suggest that we retire to the house and discuss this over a cup of tea?" Darcy said.

"Lizzy?" Mr. Phillips deferred.

She nodded. Her lips pressed together firmly. He had seen his sister do that very thing when attempting to keep her lips from trembling. His heart ached over the unfortunate circumstances in which his new neighbour found herself.

"May I escort you," Darcy offered, extending his arm to her. Georgiana would have to walk with Richard, for Miss Elizabeth looked as if she needed an arm on which to lean.

Chapter 4

"We should send for your father, Lizzy." Her uncle said once they had all entered Netherfield's drawing room. He looked to Mr. Bingley. "Is there someone who could be sent?"

"Of course, I will find someone."

Mr. Bingley seemed to be as amiable as he was handsome. Elizabeth wished she could say the same for his sisters, but she could not. They were handsome ladies, but she suspected, from their haughty looks, that their beauty was no deeper than their perfectly styled coiffeurs and finely detailed gowns.

"Are you well?" Mr. Darcy asked as he saw her to a sofa.

Elizabeth nodded but then shrugged before shaking her head. How could she be well? She had just discovered that someone she considered as a dear friend thought she needed an inheritance to tempt a gentleman to marry her.

"Perhaps we could ask the others to leave, so we could discuss this in private with Mr. Phillips?" he offered as he sat down beside her.

"No. I am well or will be." She did not want to be left in a room, with only her uncle as a chaperone and sitting on a sofa next to the handsome Mr. Darcy. And goodness! He was handsome. Dashingly handsome.

Oh, what Mr. Darcy must think of her! To hear that she needed help securing a husband was embarrassing enough. To hear that same information with an audience of strangers was... she could not think of a word that properly described the humiliation of such a thing.

"What if I did not claim my inheritance?" she asked hopefully.

"That is not an option," her uncle said. "It is already yours. The incumbrance on Netherfield is in place."

Why did she have to marry to be rid of the garden? She wanted to stamp her foot and screech at the stipulation. What if she never found anyone who she could love well enough to marry? What if no one ever loved her as she desired to be loved? There had to be a way to make this requirement less of a constraint.

"Could Mr. Bingley not just lease the estate and never purchase it? Doing so would alleviate the financial strain placed on Mr. Darcy's finances."

Miss Bingley made a soft, amused snorting sound. "Mr. Darcy's finances are well-able to sustain the expenses of this trifling estate." Her tone was one that declared quite loudly that she found Elizabeth to be ignorant.

Elizabeth drew a calming, fortifying breath. Oh, she did not like Miss Bingley! Arrogance of any sort was off-putting. However, the amount of haughtiness displayed by Miss Bingley was revolting. She allowed her eyes to sweep from Miss Bingley's hem to her face. They would see who was the more ignorant of the two of them, and Elizabeth was positive Miss Bingley would be the one to be found wanting.

"It is a pleasure to meet another lady who is as interested in estate management as I am." She pressed her lips into a thin smile and attempted to force her eyes to carry something other than the disdain she felt for Miss Bingley.

"Estate management," Mrs. Hurst said with a laugh. "Oh, dear, no. Ladies, proper ones, do not understand such things."

Elizabeth's brow furrowed as if she was truly perplexed, which she was not. She had no doubt that, other than to plan a menu, see a room decorated, or a soiree planned, Miss Bingley knew next to nothing about the many and various duties and details that went into running an estate of any size.

"Then, I must ask; how does your sister know that Mr. Darcy's finances can support an estate such as Netherfield along with any other properties and investments he possesses?"

"One has only to see Pemberley to know it," Miss Bingley replied.

"What is Pemberley?" Elizabeth was certain it was likely a large estate somewhere, but she thought it best if Miss Bingley were to know that what she held as a great status symbol was of little importance in a place where it was not known. At least, she hoped it was a place that was not known in Hertfordshire, although she suspected that her mother, her aunt, and Lady Lucas would know something about it.

"Oh, do not pretend that you have not heard how wealthy Mr. Darcy is," Mrs. Hurst said.

"We have," Charlotte said, "but I do not see how that informs us about what Pemberley is."

"It is my estate in Derbyshire," Mr. Darcy said. "It is rather grand. Impressive even."

"He is being modest," Mrs. Hurst said.

"Then, that is a mark in *his* favour." Irritation bubbled inside Elizabeth. "However, I will still maintain that one must have an intimate acquaintance with ledgers and accounts if one is to judge if another can or cannot withstand an expense being added. Many things can look quite pretty and well-presented on their exterior, and yet, they can be hiding an absence of anything of substance behind their façade." And she was not speaking only about estates!

Colonel Fitzwilliam covered a laugh with a cough, drawing her attention to him and away from Mr. Bingley's sisters. When she caught his eye, he merely flicked his eyebrows upward quickly and gave an almost imperceivable nod of his head as if he agreed with her assessment of Mrs. Hurst and Miss Bingley.

"Do you know about estate management?" Mr. Darcy asked her.

"Yes." He might as well know all of her flaws. Then, perhaps he would understand why she needed help finding someone to marry her.

"How interesting," he muttered. A small smile played at his lips. He did not seem appalled by the information.

"Not all of us know about those things," Jane said. "However, when we were young, Elizabeth showed an interest, and our father has indulged her."

Mr. Darcy's small smile grew slightly. It was almost as if he was delighted by her unusual education. At least, he did not appear to be laughing at her.

"Could we just get on with what needs to be discussed?" Miss Bingley asked.

That settled it in Elizabeth's mind. Mr. Darcy was not laughing at her but was, rather, pleased, and Miss Bingley was not.

"Do we have tea?" Colonel Fitzwilliam asked.

"It is coming," Miss Bingley replied.

"Then, so is the discussion that needs to be had," the colonel said, causing Miss Bingley's smile to curl in disgust before she caught herself.

"Your father has been summoned." Mr. Bingley took a seat close to Jane.

There was no denying that he was well on his way to falling under the spell that Jane seemed to be able to cast on all gentlemen that made them worship at her feet. It was not as if she tried to create the enchantment, it was just part of her person. Her kindness radiated from deep within, making her as attractive as she was pretty. Elizabeth had to admit that Jane and Mr. Bingley did make a handsome couple, and to have Jane settled so close to Longbourn would be wonderful.

"Can Mr. Bingley not just continue to lease?" she asked again.

"Not if he wishes to fulfill his father's wish that he become a landed gentleman," Mr. Darcy answered.

"Ah, yes, I do think I heard that your friend had ties to trade." She allowed her gaze to shift to Miss Bingley. How could that woman think she was better than every other lady in the room when her father had not been a gentleman?

"Am I right to assume it was your father who was in trade and not just those who came before him?" she asked Mr. Bingley.

"Yes. He owned some mills in the North."

"And do you own those mills now?" Jane asked.

"No, I do not. I am to purchase an estate to lift my family from their roots."

And, Elizabeth supposed, with a sigh, that he had hoped Netherfield was the estate to help him do so.

"Will you still lease Netherfield if you are unable to purchase it?" she asked.

It would be dreadful for such a handsome and wealthy gentleman, who made her sister blush as she was now, to be forced away from the area before an attachment of any strength could be formed between him and Jane.

"I likely will. At least, for the present."

And then, where would he look for an estate and how far away would that remove her dearest sister from her if Jane were so fortunate as to marry Mr. Bingley? If only Elizabeth had even one marriage prospect!

"I do not see why we should stay here if there is no hope of your purchasing the place," Mrs. Hurst said.

"You do not have to," Mr. Bingley answered her.

"You need a hostess," Mrs. Hurst protested.

"Caroline can fill the role."

"Or my mother would be delighted to join us while Georgiana is here," Colonel Fitzwilliam inserted.

"Lady Matlock? Here?" Mr. Hurst was once again sounding horrified, and the prospect of Lady Matlock being at Netherfield sounded as it if was far worse than the area not having enough gentlemen. Was he always such a disagreeable man?

"While you might find it beneath her, I am certain she would not find it so. Mr. Enfield was my father's cousin, after all."

Ah, so Colonel Fitzwilliam was the son of the Earl of Matlock, and if Elizabeth remembered correctly from what Mr. Enfield had told her, he had only his older brother as a sibling. Mr. Enfield had spoken about his family a few times when they were together. Her eyes turned to Mr. Darcy. He must be the relation whose parents had both died. How dreadful that must be.

Quite naturally, her attention turned next to Miss Darcy, who was watching her. Elizabeth smiled, and the smile was returned. She seemed to be a lovely young lady.

"We all have relations we do not visit," Mrs. Hurst said with a look for her husband that declared very well her thoughts on visiting those who she considered beneath her. To Elizabeth, the pair of Hursts seemed well-matched for pretentiousness.

"That brings us no closer to a solution that allows for Mr. Bingley to purchase Netherfield if he wishes," Elizabeth said.

"The solution is easy," Colonel Fitzwilliam countered. "You must marry."

"And whom shall I marry, Colonel?" she asked.

"Surely, there must be some gentleman in the area who would fit the position of husband."

"One does not just marry to sell a piece of land." Mary pressed her lips together as if she had not meant to say that. But Elizabeth was glad she had spoken, for, on this matter, she and Mary agreed.

"It seems she must in this case," Colonel Fitzwilliam replied.

"Why must Elizabeth sell what is hers?" Mary asked. "Miss Bingley claims that Mr. Darcy can sustain the cost of Netherfield, and he has not denied that what she says is true. Mr. Bingley needs an estate, but he does not have to have this one. Are there not other estates in England that can be purchased without encumbrance? Is my sister to sacrifice her happiness just so a gentleman wholly unrelated to her can fulfill the wish of his father?"

"No," Mr. Bingley answered. "Miss Mary's points are valid. I could find an estate that suits me just as well as this one." He cast a questioning glance at Mr. Darcy. He clearly valued the opinion of his friend.

"You have the right of it," Mr. Darcy agreed. "And there is always the hope that Miss Elizabeth could find a husband this season, and we can proceed as planned. However, if she does not, then, I will help you find another place."

"That is an excellent idea," Mrs. Hurst said just as the door to the drawing room opened for both a tea tray and Mr. Bennet to enter.

"I see that I have arrived at precisely the right time," Elizabeth's father said with a chuckle after introductions had been made and the tea was being poured. "Now, can someone tell me what this urgent meeting is about?"

"It is about my garden," Elizabeth said. "Uncle Phillips has just informed us that I cannot dispose of the garden until I have married, and then, it must either be sold to Mr. Darcy or along with the estate to someone else."

Her father leaned back in his chair and nodded slowly. "And why was that so important that I had to be called?"

"You know what Mama will be like when she discovers I have something more of value to offer a gentleman." Elizabeth pitched her voice low in an attempt to keep herself from feeling any more mortified than she already did.

"You, my daughter, have more to offer a gentleman than any piece of land could ever be worth," he assured her. "But I do see your point, and your fear is not unfounded." He turned to Mr. Darcy. "You are not attached, are you?"

One eyebrow cocked over Mr. Darcy's fine eyes. "I am not," he replied.

"Then, sir, you will need to be just as concerned as my Lizzy is."

"How so?" The question was asked with no little amount of wariness in his tone.

"My wife might not be a great scholar. However, I assure you she is well-versed in matchmaking, and it will not take her long to decipher that the best use of that piece of garden in advancing her daughter's position would be for you to marry Elizabeth."

Mr. Darcy grimaced. That was not exactly the look any lady wanted a handsome gentleman to wear when the idea of marrying her was presented. It did not matter if Elizabeth wanted to marry him or not. She did not want him to look so disturbed by the prospect that it caused his face to twist as if in pain.

"I understand."

"Are you interested?"

"Papa!" Elizabeth cried.

Her father laughed. "I jest. I would not accept anyone whom my daughter did not declare she loved most ardently." He patted her hand. "Be that as it may, my wife is not so particular, so you must be prepared."

"Or flee the area," Colonel Fitzwilliam said with a laugh.

"Aye, there is that option," Mr. Bennet agreed as he joined the colonel in laughing.

"I cannot. I promised Bingley I would stay."

"Then, we should devise a plan to appease my wife and provide my daughter with time to find a husband who will love her as she deserves." Elizabeth's father patted her hand again. "If, indeed, there is such a fellow to be found."

Elizabeth loved the way her father made her feel cherished, but it was still excessively uncomfortable to be the topic of discussion in a drawing room full of strangers – some of whom seemed ambivalent and others who seemed determined to despise her and everyone else as beneath them.

Her father sipped his tea. "We will send you with Jane to your aunt and uncle in town in December. However, there is the time between now and then which will be unpleasant for you and Mr. Darcy and his unmarried friends."

He turned his eyes to the colonel. "My wife adores a uniform and thinks all her daughters should, too. They do not, but that will make little difference to my wife's efforts. And Mr. Bingley, since you are the one hoping to purchase the estate, that would make you a good second option to Mr. Darcy."

"The colonel's father is an earl," Bingley said.

Perhaps she should take back her thought that Mr. Bingley was amiable. Did he truly have to so quickly put forward an excuse for why he should not be considered as a gentleman to be pushed in her direction? She did not want him. He was destined for

Jane, but still, it was not overly polite to try to toss her to the side with such haste, now was it?

"Well, now, a lord as a relation and a uniform? Mr. Darcy might find himself second on the list when my wife discovers that bit of information." Mr. Bennet chuckled.

"Papa, please," Elizabeth begged as she glanced at the colonel, who appeared to not be listening at all but was rather in deep contemplation. "I can withstand Mama's machinations. I have for years."

Just then, the colonel clapped his hands, startling Elizabeth.

"I know just the thing that we need," he cried with great glee. "A house party! We must have a house party, Bingley. Surely we can come up with a selection of gentlemen for Miss Elizabeth – a few from town and some from here."

He leaned forward. Every fiber of his being seemed to radiate excitement as he laid out his scheme. "We will pose it as a welcoming party for Mr. Bingley to the area, a celebration of his new home for his friends from town, and a way to meet some of the notable gentlemen and ladies of the area."

He nodded as if thoroughly pleased with himself. "I will ask my mother to come to keep everything perfectly acceptable and to lend a degree of honor to the event. And Darcy, Bingley, and I will help Miss Elizabeth find a husband or whittle down her choices."

"No, no, no," Elizabeth protested. She had no desire to be the subject of such an elaborate matchmaking plan. Her mother's promotion of her, she could withstand – not happily, but it was not impossible to tolerate it. But this? This stratagem to have three handsome strangers shuffling and sorting gentlemen on her behalf was beyond what was bearable.

"It might be fun," Charlotte said.

"You cannot be serious?"

"I have never been to a house party," Jane added.

Was everyone against her?

"I have no desire to attend one," Mary said.

Well, there was one who was on her side.

"I have heard far too many tales about the untoward things that can happen at such events," Mary added.

"They are not all full of debauchery," the colonel teased her. "Come now, Miss Mary. My mother will be here to act as a chaperone, and I assure you that she is not one to allow anything improper. Am I not right, Darcy?"

"You are, but a house party?"

"You see," Elizabeth grasped desperately at any straw of hope that being subjected to the matchmaking schemes of three gentlemen and her mother could be avoided. "Mr. Darcy does not want to have a house party, and this is his house."

"Actually," Mr. Bingley said with a sly smile, "I am the master of Netherfield at present, and I find the idea of a house party to be delightful."

"The papers have not been signed." Mr. Darcy sounded nearly as desperate as Elizabeth felt.

"I believe I attempted to use that excuse earlier today, and do you know what I was told?"

Mr. Darcy's eyes narrowed, and his jaw clenched. Evidently, Elizabeth was correct. Mr. Bingley was not all amiability.

"Yes." The answer was given in a reluctant tone and with a shake of Mr. Darcy's head. "If Bingley wants a house party, he can have one, but I may not be in attendance. I have my sister to see to. She is not yet out."

"Mother will be here," Colonel Fitzwilliam said. "Georgiana will be safe. You know Mother is not going to let you escape a party until you are married." He rubbed his hands together as if thoroughly delighted with his plan.

"Miss Lucas and Miss Bennet, since you two seem to be the most agreeable ladies to this scheme, perhaps you could make a list of area gentlemen and ladies we could possibly invite, and tomorrow, we can discuss them over another cup of tea. Miss Bingley and Mrs. Hurst, you will, of course, be allowed to suggest a gentleman or two from town who might interest Miss Bingley. Added to that, you must see that the house is prepared to receive the countess and our guests. Darcy, Bingley, and I will devise our own list of possible guests."

He rose. "It has been a most successful meeting."

No one said a word but simply stared after Colonel Fitzwilliam as he left the room.

"I like him," Mr. Bennet said as he rose from his place.

"He does have a commanding and detail-oriented way about him," Uncle Philips agreed. "Mr. Darcy, would you like to go over the details of your relation's will now, or would another time be better?"

"Now seems as good a time as any. Bingley, can we use your study?"

"Of course."

Mr. Darcy turned to Elizabeth. "Can I call for my carriage to take you home?"

"That would be lovely," Jane answered before Elizabeth could protest that it would be a bad idea to arrive home in the carriage belonging to a wealthy, unmarried gentleman who needed her garden before he could sell his estate.

"Until tomorrow, then," he bowed and took his leave of the room.

"I will wait for the carriage outside." She refused to listen to any protests or feel the disapproving looks of Miss Bingley or Mrs. Hurst. She needed fresh air, a long walk, and a way to turn back time so she could convince Mr. Enfield that he should not leave anything to her, for his stipulations were only destined to make her loathe a place she once loved.

Chapter 5

Later that evening, Darcy settled into a chair in Netherfield's library with a glass of port at his side and Mr. Enfield's journal in his lap. This well-worn book had been part of a small crate of possessions that Mr. Phillips had delivered to Darcy after going over the particulars of the will with him. The things in that box were ones which Mr. Enfield had specifically outlined were to remain Darcy's possessions even after the estate was sold – if it was to be sold at all.

Mr. Enfield had certainly loved Netherfield and the area in which it sat. Darcy cast a gaze out the window at the lengthening shadows created by a late summer sunset. Orange and pink-tinged the clouds and bathed the hills in the distance in their warm parting glow.

Enfield had most certainly had good reason to prize such beauty.

Darcy looked at the bookcases that were only half-filled with books. Prize possessions of all sorts stood in the empty places. Enfield had often picked up one or another of the items and recited some story that was attached to it. His ability to weave a story in front of the fire had been something Darcy looked forward to during his short visits with Enfield. The man was entertaining but not in the attention-seeking fashion some were. He preferred small audiences and quiet spaces. This room was a fine example of that. There was room here for no more than a half dozen people to sit with any comfort.

"What are you reading?" Georgiana asked. She had already been seated in here with a book when Darcy had arrived. Somehow, they had both managed to retire here without being joined by Miss Bingley or Mrs. Hurst. Neither of them would be so fortunate for long, he supposed, but he would enjoy the pleasantness while it was available.

"This is one of Mr. Enfield's journals," he said in answer to his sister's inquiry.

"How interesting." She closed the book she held. "Is it completely private, or could you read it to me?"

"There were no instructions about my not sharing the journals. I was only told that I must keep them when I sell the house. I suppose it is so Mr. Enfield's story can be remembered for generations in his family."

"I like that," his sister said. "I only met him twice, but he always struck me as an admirable gentleman. I was not wrong in that assessment, was I?"

"Not at all. Mr. Wickham was a cad who purposefully deceived you. The fault in deciphering his character is not due to your lack of discernment, but rather to his ability to know how to bend and twist himself to keep his true intent hidden."

"But it remains that I was deceived by him and could be deceived by others."

She had a point, and as much as Darcy disliked the idea of agreeing with her about this, he had to. "Not everyone is so intent upon doing harm."

"But so many do hide themselves." Her eyes flicked to the door, and she lowered her voice to a whisper. "Miss Bingley plays at being what she thinks you would want in a wife, but then, that is how many of the ladies I have met tend to be. They are what they need to be to snare the best situation for themselves. I have never liked that, and I am certain I could not pretend to be what I am not for all the money in the world." Her brow furrowed. "But then, I do not lack for anything. Perhaps if I did, I would think otherwise?"

"Your heart is noble," Darcy replied with a smile. "I do not think you could be what you are not even in the most trying circumstances." Her heart was too tender to be callous and calculating – at least, he hoped it still was. "Your ordeal with Mr. Wickham has not made you harden your heart against the world, has it?"

She shook her head. "Not all of it, or not completely, that is. It has, however, made me more wary of the world."

"It has done the same for me." And he had been wary of the world for some time, so the deepening of that sentiment was no small thing.

"Do not apologize for that," he added when she opened her mouth to speak. "I would like to think that those feelings of guardedness will only prove to make both you and me wise. That is, they will as long as we do not succumb to only feeling trepidation instead of using the hard experience we have been through to filter what was see and know."

"I like that thought," she said with a smile. "I have felt foolish for several weeks now. It is pleasant to think that my foolishness could result in wisdom."

"You are no fool," Darcy assured her. "I have had enough seasons in town to know what a foolish lady is, and you are not that."

"I hope to remain so well-thought-of by you."

He held out his hand to her, and when she placed her hand in his, he gave it a squeeze. "I could never think ill of you."

"Nor I of you," she replied.

"That does not mean that we cannot occasionally disagree and be put out with one another."

"Oh, I most heartily agree." She laughed.

He opened the journal he held. "Shall we see if this is something that I can read to you without being too indelicate or some such thing?" It was a journal, after all. These were Mr. Enfield's private ruminations which, Darcy was certain, had not been filtered for public consumption.

"Yes, please." Georgiana released his hand and made a show of getting comfortable in her seat. Ever since she was a baby, she had always loved being read to. The thought that he was the one to provide her this pleasure made him glad.

"This one is dated May, five years ago." His brow furrowed. "I think I had visited him just before this on my way to Rosings for Easter." He settled back into his chair, took a sip of his wine, and began reading.

"The garden is bursting with new life. Just today, Miss Elizabeth and I found some new shoots poking through the soil in the far section of the garden that borders the wildwood between here and Longbourn. While admiring these new shoots, Miss Elizabeth told me that she is to be out this year. She is young, much like these plants will be in a few weeks' time, but I think she is ready to set her bloom and display her charm to the world. She is not like some of the other young ladies I have met. Miss Elizabeth has a quick wit and is in no rush to marry – much to her mother's dismay, I am given to know. I chuckle even now remembering the roll of Miss Elizabeth's eyes as she told me about her mother's desire to see both she and Miss Bennet soon married. I say good luck to Mrs. Bennet! Those two ladies are destined for more than an assembly in Meryton can bring them. Ah, but, Miss Elizabeth's addition to the numbers that attend the soirees in the area will be lovely. I think very highly of her. If I had been fortunate enough to have married and had children, I would have hoped for a daughter exactly like her.

Darcy stopped reading. "What follows is a list of the flowers that are in bloom, which I will not read unless you wish it." He looked at his sister, who shook her head.

"Miss Elizabeth could not have been very old when she came out," she said before he could begin reading again.

"No, she must not have been. How old do you suppose she is now?" Darcy had thought that very thing about Miss Elizabeth's age as he was reading the entry.

"I am not sure. However, she is younger than Miss Bennet, and Miss Bennet looks to be about Miss Bingley's age."

"Are you thinking then that Miss Elizabeth is less than twenty?" He had thought she looked more womanly than girlish. Though her figure was slight, he had found it temptingly womanly if he were to be honest with himself.

Georgiana shrugged. "She might be, but she is older than Miss Mary who looks like she is at least eighteen."

"She must be twenty." For he could not fathom a father like Mr. Bennet, who seemed to adore his daughter, putting her out at fourteen. Fifteen was early, but it was not so early that he had never heard of it being done before.

"She seems nice."

Darcy nodded as he prepared to read more. "She does."

"I think she would make a good friend."

Darcy turned surprised eyes to his sister. "You do?"

She nodded. "I like her, though I do not know why. So do not ask me."

He eyed his sister for a minute. He would dearly like to know what it was about Miss Elizabeth that called to her. Georgiana never gave her approbation about someone so quickly and on such a short acquaintance. Not even when it had come to Wickham, and since that incident with Wickham, he would have expected her to be even more apprehensive.

"I thought you said you were wary about the world."

"I am."

"Then, how can you say you like Miss Elizabeth without knowing your reasons for saying so?"

"How could I say I do not like her without provocation to dislike her? Is it not better for me to like her until I see a reason to change my opinion?"

The door opened before Darcy could reply. Thankfully, it was neither Miss Bingley nor Mrs. Hurst who entered.

"What are you two doing?" Richard asked.

"Reading," Darcy replied.

"And talking about Miss Elizabeth," Georgiana added.

"She seems to be a lovely young lady." Richard lowered himself into a chair. "It is a hard place she has been put in, and she has borne it with dignity."

"I am sure I would have dissolved into a puddle of tears if I were her," Georgiana said.

"I am surprised she is allowing us to push the idea of marriage." Richard rubbed the back of his neck. "I wonder why."

"You did not give her much of a chance to oppose your scheme." Darcy was less than pleased with his cousin's commandeering of the whole situation and his seeming lack of feeling for the position into which he was forcing Miss Elizabeth.

"That was purposefully done. I will be interested to see what she has to say tomorrow when we begin the process of creating invitations."

"Are you testing her?" Darcy asked in surprise. He should have known his cousin was up to something Machiavellian, for his schemes often had a purpose other than the one stated.

Richard nodded.

"Why?"

"Allow me to ask you a few questions that I will not be sharing with anyone else in this house." He gave each of them a quick, pointed look before continuing. "Why did Enfield leave her a portion of his land?" He held up one finger. "Did the uncle have anything to do with that? It is convenient that he was Enfield's solicitor." He held up a second finger. "Secondly, why does she need help finding a husband? She is not lacking in handsomeness. Is it a lack of gentlemen or is there something about her or her ambitions that keep her from it?"

"You are very skeptical!" Georgiana cried.

Darcy had to agree. Of course, he had also wondered a few of the things Richard had mentioned.

Georgiana snatched the journal from Darcy and read *"If I had been fortunate enough to have married and had children, I would have hoped for a daughter like her."* Then, she handed the journal back to Darcy. "I think that answers at least one of your questions."

"What is that?" Richard leaned forward to view the book Darcy now held.

"One of the journals that Mr. Enfield left to me," Darcy answered.

"And am I to believe that is what he said about Miss Elizabeth?"

"Yes." Georgiana had her arms folded defensively across her chest.

"Then, she ingratiated herself to him."

"For what purpose?" Darcy kept his tone nonchalant with some difficulty. He was feeling a great deal like Georgiana looked – provoked.

Richard shrugged and stretched out his legs, crossing them at the ankle. "I am not certain, but the possibility has to be considered."

"Why?" Georgiana demanded. "Why must we think ill of her just because Mr. Enfield liked her, and she is pretty but not married?"

Richard's eyebrows rose high.

"Georgiana likes Miss Elizabeth," Darcy explained.

"Why?" Richard asked.

"Why should she not?" Darcy replied.

"I suppose there is no reason not to, but I also think we must do our duty in ascertaining if she is worthy of Georgiana's admiration."

"And yet, you propose introducing her to a gathering of gentlemen and ladies before you know if she is worthy of their admiration," Darcy countered.

The idea that Richard would call Miss Elizabeth's honour into question made Darcy bristle for some reason, and truthfully, there was no reason for his irritable reaction other than he, like Georgiana, liked her, though not as a gentleman admired a lady. He had only just met her. He liked her as a person. Just as a person. And as a possible friend for his sister. A respected acquaintance. There, that was what she was. Miss Elizabeth was a respected acquaintance.

"How else am I to evaluate if it is a lack of gentlemen or a deficiency in her character?"

"You could take a trip to the village or visit a few neighbours. I am certain there is a gossip somewhere in the area who could fill you in on all the details you think you need to know."

Richard chuckled. "I am certain I could do those things, but a house party sounded like a great deal more fun."

No, it did not. At least, it did not sound that way to Darcy.

"Who shall we invite for you?" Georgiana asked.

"Me?" Richard said in surprise. "This party is not for me."

"Your mother might see it otherwise," Darcy inserted.

"My mother often sees things that are not true when they are about me and marriage," Richard retorted. "And you heard Mr. Bennet. If I do not provide Miss Elizabeth with a selection of eligible bachelors, then, I along with you, Darcy, will be the object of her mother's scheming. I prefer to attack before being attacked."

Darcy chuckled. "And yet, you have set yourself up to be attacked from all sides – by your mother and hers."

He turned his eyes back to the journal he held. They had discussed Miss Elizabeth enough. He did not want to hear about any more plans to see her wed or how they must watch her carefully for signs of duplicity. Where was this Richard when they were hiring Mrs. Younge? A bit more skepticism then would have been good.

Darcy arranged himself to begin reading and considered that perhaps the ordeal with Wickham was partially to blame for Richard's current suspicion of a new acquaintance for Georgiana. He supposed he could not fault him for that.

"This is dated two days later," he began, *"Young Sam was once again caught out by Mr. Franklin's dog when taking a shortcut to town, and once again, thankfully, the beast only growled and threatened..."*

Chapter 6

SEPTEMBER 5, 1811

"Oh, my, he is handsome, is he not?"

It was the third time Elizabeth's mother had whispered that question to her since they had arrived at Netherfield to go over the proposed list of people to invite to the husband-finding party that Colonel Fitzwilliam insisted upon having.

"And an earl's son," her mother added in her same non-discrete whisper.

"Younger son, Mama," Mary corrected.

"You cannot tell me that any son of an earl is a pauper for I simply will not believe it."

"Even if it is true?" Mary asked.

"Is it true?" Mrs. Bennet's eyes grew wide, and her admiration of Colonel Fitzwilliam morphed into something more cunningly assessing.

"I do not know," Mary replied. "Shall I ask him?"

"I should think not!" Mrs. Bennet cried as Elizabeth bit back a smile. Mary was becoming more and more adept at provoking their mother with very direct and matter-of-fact opinions and questions.

"Is there an issue with the list?" the colonel asked. He had just handed a list of names to Jane who was seated between Elizabeth and their mother.

Mrs. Bennet blinked and blushed. "No, no, there is nothing wrong with your list. Is there, Jane?"

"I honestly could not tell you," Jane replied. "I think it is best if Elizabeth decides that."

"Elizabeth will say there is something wrong with all of them." Mrs. Bennet snatched the paper from Jane.

Elizabeth clenched her teeth together to keep the retort she wanted to give from flying from her mouth. The thing that was wrong was that she was being forced to attend a party where the guest list was specifically filled with gentlemen who were to be pushed at her.

"And why is that, madame?" Colonel Fitzwilliam settled onto the sofa across from Mrs. Bennet in Netherfield's sitting room. His expression was all seriousness. If he was laughing at her and, by extension, the rest of the Bennets gathered, Elizabeth saw no sign of it.

"Why is that?" her mother repeated.

"Yes, why would Miss Elizabeth find something wrong with all the suggestions on that list." He waved to the paper Mrs. Bennet held. "I have included the pertinent information – name, age, title if there is one, occupation if there is one, current income as far as it is circulated, and any future possible increase to income or fortune."

Mrs. Bennet scanned the list. "It is very thorough," she muttered.

"Is there any other way to make a list than thoroughly?" the colonel asked.

"I do not see yourself, Mr. Darcy, or Mr. Bingley on this list," Mary said.

"That is because we do not need invitations since we are already here."

"But would not that information help my mother decide who would be the best match for my sister?" Mary levelled a challenging look at the colonel.

"The information is irrelevant."

"Are you saying, then, that you, along with your cousin and friend, are not to be considered?" Mary asked.

The colonel looked a trifle uneasy at that question but after a moment's pause answered. "I suppose that is what it means."

"Is that because my sister is beneath your notice?"

Mary had been in quite the state yesterday when they had returned home to tell their mother about the party that was being planned on Elizabeth's behalf. She could not or would not let go of her objection to the fact that Elizabeth was required to give up her garden and that she had to marry to do so. *I do not see why Mr. Darcy does not have to marry before he can sell his portion of the estate!* she had said more than once.

"No, no, that is not it at all." Colonel Fitzwilliam shifted uneasily. "It is just that none of us require a wife at present."

"And these gentlemen on your list do?"

His eyes narrowed the tiniest bit. "Yes."

"Indeed?" Mary's tone let everyone know that she did not believe the colonel's answer.

"Every gentleman eventually needs a wife," Mrs. Bennet said with a smile for the colonel.

"Mr. Enfield did not have a wife." Mary's comment drew a small huff and a reproving look from their mother.

"I am simply stating a fact."

"I believe it is a fact of which we need not be reminded," their mother replied. "I see nothing wrong with any of these choices."

"But you have still not told me why your daughter would find them wanting." Colonel Fitzwilliam was persistent.

"May I see the list Mama?" Elizabeth asked.

Once she had received it, she gave the paper a cursory glance. The colonel's handwriting was very neat, even if it was a bit small and close, and all the information that Colonel Fitzwilliam had said was there, was there.

"Based on this information, I cannot say if there is anything lacking in any of these gentlemen for it does not tell me what I need to know." She held the list out to the colonel.

"How can it not?" he asked in surprise as he took the paper from her.

"The details listed quantify and qualify a gentleman based merely on what he does and his possessions. What about his character? What about annoying habits or endearing qualities? What does that paper tell me about those things? Financial stability is important, but it does not trump affection, respect, and nobleness of character."

The room fell silent. Elizabeth was certain her mother was not even breathing for she had heard her suck in a breath when Elizabeth had said there was something more valuable than fortune.

Colonel Fitzwilliam's lips tipped up on the right side into a half-smile. "That is well said, but those things cannot be ascertained without your meeting these gentlemen."

Elizabeth looked at Jane and then back to Colonel Fitzwilliam. "That is both true and why I am resigned to attending this party."

She could sacrifice herself on Jane's behalf. Last night, when the candle was burning low in their room, Jane had confessed her interest in Mr. Bingley. While this party might not produce a match for Elizabeth, it might for Jane.

"Resigned?" The colonel scowled.

"Yes, resigned. This is what must be done so, please, just get on with it." She took a folded piece of paper from her reticule and held it out to him. "These are our suggestions for whom to invite from the area."

Her heart sighed as he took it from her. No one on that list was the sort of gentleman she wanted to marry. They were fine, upstanding men, but they did not engage her heart.

"When is this party to start?" she asked.

"Can it not be avoided altogether?" Mr. Darcy said.

"How can it be?" Elizabeth asked. "I need to marry so you can dispose of your inheritance."

"But I do not need to do it immediately." He gave his cousin a withering glare.

It was comforting to Elizabeth. to know that she was not the only one, other than Mary, who did not want to attend a house party.

"I was thinking that it could commence just after Michaelmas."

Apparently, the colonel was not affected by his cousin's words or glare.

"That should give us time," he continued, "to get the invitations sent and for our guests to reply with their delight or regrets."

"And there will be much to prepare," Mrs. Bennet said. "It is no small thing to organize meals and soirees to entertain such a large group of people. It will be a fortnight in length, will it not? I cannot imagine that one week will be enough for Elizabeth to decide on whom to marry."

"There may not be a gentleman there for me," Elizabeth inserted quickly. In her mother's mind, this party was going to be her answer to prayer. According to her, three of her daughters would be happily settled on a gentleman by its conclusion.

"There will be if you are willing to find one."

"It is not that I am unwilling, Mama," she protested softly.

"We should begin with writing the invitations," Jane interjected before their mother could say anything further. "That is the most pressing element, is it not?"

"Miss Bingley and Mrs. Hurst will see to that," Colonel Fitzwilliam said.

Elizabeth hoped the colonel checked the invitations to make certain they were sent out as he instructed. She did not trust either Miss Bingley or Mrs. Hurst.

"Bingley will sign and post them," he continued.

That was excellent news. She was almost certain she could trust Mr. Bingley not to do something cruel.

Colonel Fitzwilliam stood. "It has been a successful meeting."

"What about entertainment and food?" Mrs. Bennet said.

"My mother will approve whatever set of events is suggested by Bingley." He turned toward the door and then back. "This is a party to welcome Bingley to the neighbourhood. That is the blanket it wears. We are not broadcasting this as a *Marry Miss Elizabeth* party."

"Richard!" Darcy snapped.

Elizabeth rose. "If you will excuse me, Colonel, Mama, I do not believe I am needed for anything further."

She balled her hands into fists at her side. The action was more effective when one did not wear gloves as the material of the gloves prevented the sharpness of her nails pressing into her palms from distracting her from her overwhelming emotions.

"We have not yet had tea," the colonel said. "I was just going to call for it."

"I do not require any. Thank you." She dipped a curtsey and willed her feet to carry her calmly from the room rather than running as she wished to do.

A *Marry Miss Elizabeth party*? She shook her head at the name as she skipped down Netherfield's steps and headed towards her garden, crossing the lawn at a quick pace. The faster she could get away from the house the better. Tears stung her eyes, but she blinked them away instead of letting them fall. She could do this. Jane deserved a chance to see if she and Mr. Bingley were a good match, and this party would give them an excellent opportunity to discover that.

Of course, if Elizabeth did not find a match for herself, she knew that Jane would be moving away from her, but that could not be helped. Jane deserved happiness even if it came at her expense.

"Miss Elizabeth," Miss Darcy greeted her as she entered her garden, "I hope you do not mind that I am visiting your garden." She had risen from the bench on which she had been sitting.

"No, not at all." Elizabeth motioned for her to be seated.

"I needed some quiet," she explained, "and Mrs. Annesley thought that a wander around the garden would be good for me."

"Who is Mrs. Annesley?" Elizabeth asked as she settled on the bench next to Miss Darcy.

"My companion. She is quite lovely."

"That is good to hear." Elizabeth wondered what it was like to have a hired companion rather than a sister to keep a lady company.

"I can see why you liked this part of the garden," Miss Darcy continued. "It is peaceful and has such a beautiful aspect of the house, gardens, and surrounding lands."

That was precisely what Elizabeth liked about this spot. "It is an excellent place to order one's thoughts." She drew and released a deep breath.

"Forgive me for being forward," Miss Darcy said, "but you do not look well."

"My spirit just needs some bolstering," Elizabeth said with a forced smile. "Life does not get easier as one gets older." She sighed. It was a pity that it did not, but it was not a surprise.

"Will you be sorry to part with this garden?" The question was spoken softly and in a tentative tone.

"That is a good question." She glanced at the young woman sitting next to her. Miss Darcy could not be much older than her youngest sisters, but there was a seriousness in her expression and welcoming air about her that made her seem older.

"Yesterday, before I met you, I would have said yes, but today?" Elizabeth shook her head. "Honestly? I regret ever having seen this garden." She blinked as rapidly as she could, but it was of no use. The tears would not be contained, and she was forced to seek her handkerchief.

"Is that because of the need to marry to sell it?"

Elizabeth nodded but then, shook her head again.

"Then, it is the party."

"Yes." She dried her eyes again. There was no need for tears her mind told her heart, but her heart did not agree.

"May I ask you something personal?" Miss Darcy turned towards her.

"Perhaps."

"I would promise you that I would not tell a soul what your answer is, but I have promised my brother that I will not keep secrets from him. Therefore, if he were to ask me, I would have to tell him, but I would not tell anyone else."

Elizabeth smiled. "It sounds as if you and your brother are close."

"We are." Miss Darcy paused. "May I ask?"

This young lady was excessively considerate and well-mannered. Elizabeth nodded.

"Why are you not married? You are very pretty and smart. Do you not want to marry?"

"Thank you. I appreciate your compliments." Elizabeth drew another deep breath and released it. "It is not that I do not want to marry. I would like very much to have my own home and children. However, I do not want to have those things so much that I am willing to accept just any offer."

"Have you had an offer?"

Elizabeth held Miss Darcy's gaze. "You must not tell my mother, but yes. Only my father and I know about that offer. He was not an unworthy gentleman in any way. In fact, he had a promising future, but he was not for me. I did not love him as anything more than a friend, and he has since found someone who does love him as he deserved to be loved."

She looked away from Miss Darcy and back toward Netherfield's house. A handsome gentleman with a sister, who, Elizabeth guessed, adored him, was making his way toward them.

"Maybe I was foolish to refuse him," she continued. "Maybe I will never find someone who will stir my heart as I wish for it to be stirred. However, I am too young to give up on my dream just yet." She smiled at Miss Darcy. "I want a husband who respects me and who can be my confidant. I want someone to whom I can turn in good times and bad and who will help me be the best me I can be. If he is all those things, then, I think he will also be a good father."

"Georgiana, Miss Elizabeth." Mr. Darcy gave a bow of his head in greeting. "May I join you?"

"You may," Elizabeth said.

"Are you well?" he asked her.

"I am." At least, she was better than she had been. Whether or not she would feel truly well anytime soon was remained to be seen. "A few minutes of fresh air, quiet, and a friend with whom to talk was just what I needed."

"I must apologize for my cousin."

Elizabeth shook her head. "Please, I have just begun to forget his words."

"Was Richard rude?" Miss Darcy's tone was filled with incredulity.

"I doubt it was purposefully done," Elizabeth assured her.

One of Mr. Darcy's eyebrows arched as if he was not so certain it was so innocent.

"You do not think so?" she asked him.

"I believe it was not cruelly done. I believe he meant to arrest your mother's attention."

"I am certain he succeeded."

"What did he say?" Miss Darcy whispered.

"He referred to the party as a *Marry Miss Elizabeth* party." The words still stung, but knowing that Mr. Darcy found them inappropriate helped dampen the sharp prick that repeating them brought to her heart.

"How dreadful!" Miss Darcy cried. "I am surprised you did not shed more tears than you did." She placed a hand on Elizabeth's. "However, we know one thing for certain, my cousin is not the gentleman for you. I will not even allow you to consider him."

Elizabeth wrapped her hand around Miss Darcy's. "If you were out, I would ask you to stand by my side through this party so you could help me decipher whom to choose and whom to avoid." She shifted her eyes to Mr. Darcy. "You have a very wise and compassionate sister."

"I will not dispute that," he agreed. "Now, what shall we discuss?"

"Anything but marriage and house parties," Elizabeth said with a laugh.

Chapter 7

SEPTEMBER 7, 1811

"Mr. Darcy?"

Darcy turned toward the familiar voice that greeted him. "Miss Elizabeth." He removed his hat and bowed. "It is a pleasant morning, is it not?"

"Excessively." Her smile lit her captivating eyes, and he was again struck by her beauty just as he had been upon their first meeting in her garden at Netherfield.

"In fact," she continued, "according to my sisters, it is a perfect day to walk into Meryton. They are all meeting me here soon."

"Since I have enjoyed my walk, I would say your sisters may indeed be correct." He motioned for her to return to her place of repose on a stile while he found a place to lean against the fence. "What takes you to Meryton today?"

"Ribbons, lace, and a dressmaker. It seems I am not only going to be subjected to attending a party, but also the improvement of my wardrobe."

He studied her face. She did not seem displeased with the idea of improving her wardrobe even though her words seemed to imply it. "I am not certain if I should give you my congratulations or condolences," he replied honestly.

She laughed. "I am not certain which I would like to receive, sir, but I will thank you for your concern anyway." One of her hands smoothed her skirt. "I am not opposed to adding new dresses to my wardrobe, nor do I dread selecting ribbons and lace for embellishments and bonnets. However, the reason for all of it is still unsettling even if I am beginning to feel a bit more at ease about the party."

He desperately hated that she was being forced to do what she did not wish to do.

"You do know that I could find another tenant," he said. "This party does not have to happen."

He had spent the greater share of a day and a half feeling uneasy about being in any way a source of Miss Elizabeth's tears in the garden two days ago.

"In fact, I could keep the estate without a tenant," he suggested.

"I appreciate your generosity, and your concern for me does you credit." Her eyes sparkled with amusement. "You have earned Mary's approbation with your hesitance to require a party. She was not favourably disposed to you before our last meeting at Netherfield, but your question about avoiding having a party lifted you in her eyes. Her opinions are not easily swayed, so I must congratulate you on your success."

Darcy turned his hat around on its brim as he continued to watch Miss Elizabeth's animated features. Her eyes and mouth were so expressive. Her face was well-proportioned, and she had a small dimple that made an appearance on her right cheek when she smiled.

"You are determined then that this party must move forward? I truly would not be disappointed if it were not to happen at all. I am not a social fellow."

"Is it, then, your own comfort and not mine that makes you offer to keep Netherfield?" Her eyes were still sparkling.

"Not at all. I am keenly aware that you do not wish for it, and I cannot help feeling dreadful that I am the cause of your discomfort." His eyes moved from looking at her to examining his hat. "Georgiana told me that you regret having ever seen your garden."

That, accompanied by the remembrance of tears in Miss Elizabeth's eyes and a handkerchief clutched in her hand, had pierced his heart.

The pretty young lady on the stile drew a deep breath and released it. "It is true in part."

"Only in part?" Curiosity rose within him. "Why only in part?"

"There might be some good to come from this ordeal."

"How so?"

"There is the chance that I might find a husband."

Was that a good thing? He supposed it would be if she were truly happy.

"But that is not why you have agreed to go along with my cousin's plans, is it?"

A lady who wished to find a husband did not resign herself to being presented with a selection of gentleman, from which to pick a husband, as if it were a sentence handed down by the magistrate. At least, as far as he could tell from what he had seen of society and the marriage mart, she did not.

"No," Miss Elizabeth replied, "but it is a possibility that I must consider as a positive outcome."

Darcy shifted his weight from one leg to the other and rested one hand on top of the fence against which he leaned. "What, pray tell, is your true reason for not allowing me to call off the house party?"

"I am not certain I should say." She stood. "And since my sisters are almost here, I cannot say."

Darcy turned his head to look in the direction Elizabeth was looking. There in the distance were four young ladies walking in their direction.

"They are not so close that they would hear," he said.

She chuckled softly. "I had not taken you to be such a curious gentleman."

"I am not always so, but at times…"

"Such as now?"

"Yes." How could he not be curious about what she was thinking? Miss Elizabeth had not once conducted herself as any other young lady he had ever met. Oh, she was all that was proper – she was not different in that regard and he was not questioning her character. It was just that she was simply different, and she interested him.

"I fear you will not think well of me if I tell you." She cast a glance toward her approaching sisters. "And my sister may not thank me for telling you."

Darcy's brow furrowed. So, it had something to do with one of her sisters, did it? But which one? Was it Miss Bennet or Miss Mary? He had not met the other two Miss Bennets, and they were not invited to the party, so it could not be one of them.

"A sister must see to her sister's happiness when and where she can," she said.

"So must a brother."

It had to be Miss Bennet because Miss Mary was opposed to the idea of the party and attending would not make her happy.

"And I am certain you would not reveal your sister's secrets to a new acquaintance without a good reason."

"No, I would not." His head tipped. Miss Bennet had a secret? One that would be aided by attending a house party at Netherfield.

His breath caught in his chest as a possible secret crept into his mind. Surely, Miss Bennet was not interested in him. He had seen no sign of it if she were. There had been no notable preference for him. Indeed, he had hoped she might prefer his friend since Bingley seemed to be smitten with her beauty.

"Are you well, Mr. Darcy?" Miss Elizabeth asked.

He blinked. "Yes, yes, I am well."

Miss Elizabeth did not look convinced.

"Your sister is not..." Oh, how did one ask this without seeming arrogant? "Miss Bennet is not thinking..." he pointed to himself since he was unable to get the words out.

"What? No!" Miss Elizabeth cried.

Darcy expelled a relieved breath. "That is excellent news."

Miss Elizabeth folded her arms and glared at him. "Is Jane not handsome enough for you? Or is that she is not an heiress?"

His eyes grew wide. "No. I assure you, that is not it." He glanced toward Miss Elizabeth's sisters. They were nearly close enough now to hear his discussion with their sister. "My friend..." he whispered.

A smile suffused Miss Elizabeth's countenance. "Does he like her?"

"I believe he does."

"Thank you, Mr. Darcy."

His brow furrowed. "For what?"

"For giving me a reason to look forward to Mr. Bingley's house party."

Understanding seemed to be dawning. At least, he hoped he understood her now. "Does she like him?"

"I cannot say."

Maybe she could not say in words, but the delight in her expression answered clearly enough. It seemed

Bingley's admiration was returned. Of course, that should not surprise him. Bingley found many ladies to like and who liked him in return. Not that any of those ladies had even once caused Bingley to talk about marriage. Maybe Miss Bennet would be the lady to finally capture Bingley's yet untouched heart.

"Good day, Mr. Darcy," Miss Bennet greeted as she and her sisters approached. "Are you going to town?"

"No, I was just roaming the countryside. I never had a chance to do so on any of my visits to Netherfield before. I have toured it on horseback, but never on foot. I was about to turn back when I came upon your sister."

"Elizabeth is a great walker," Miss Bennet said. "In fact, it is because she was taking a short walk that we are meeting here instead of leaving the house together."

Miss Elizabeth had taken a walk before walking to the village? She truly must be a lover of walking.

"Solitary strolls are great sources of tranquility," Miss Elizabeth explained.

"I agree." In fact, it had been listening to Caroline, Louisa, and Hurst going on and on about how their friends from town should not be forced to mix with people from the country that had driven him from the house today in search of some quiet.

"That gives you two things you have in common," Miss Mary said. "Neither you nor Lizzy want to have a house party, and you both like walking. Are you also an avid reader?"

"I am."

"Then that makes three ways in which you are alike," she said with a smile.

"And do you like reading and walking, Miss Mary?" he asked.

"Not as much as Lizzy does, but yes, I do."

"Then, you and I also have three things in common, do we not?"

"Quite right," she agreed. She was not as soft in the way she spoke or carried herself as her two older sisters were, but he liked her. He doubted there was ever a time when Miss Mary Bennet was less than forthcoming.

"Will you allow me to introduce you to our youngest sisters?" Miss Bennet interrupted when one of those younger sisters gave Miss Bennet's arm a tap.

"Of course."

The introductions were made, a few questions were answered, and then, Miss Bennet said it was time to move on because they had much to accomplish.

He watched as she herded her three youngest sisters toward Meryton like a well-skilled shepherdess gently guiding her sheep. She was quiet and pretty, but she was no milquetoast.

Miss Elizabeth peeked over her shoulder at him. She was no milquetoast either. She was something far stronger and far more interesting than her older sister. Whomever she decided to marry was going to be a very fortunate fellow, for while Miss Elizabeth possessed a strong character, she also had a tender heart. She had to have. She was putting herself in a place she did not want to be simply for the benefit of her sister. It was something he would do for Georgiana.

Placing his hat back on his head, he turned toward Netherfield.

Miss Elizabeth was just the sort of lady he would want Georgiana to have as a sister. Or friend, he corrected quickly as he turned to look at the figures of the five Bennet ladies once more. His gaze came to rest on Miss Elizabeth and remained there for several minutes before he continued his walk. She most certainly was intriguing.

~*~

"That was a long walk," Richard commented when Darcy finally returned to the drawing room at

Netherfield.

"It is a beautiful day." Darcy arranged himself in a comfortable chair near his cousin and as far away from Bingley's sisters as he could. "I came upon the Miss Bennets while I was out." He opened Mr. Enfield's journal. "All five of them."

"Indeed?" Richard leaned forward with some interest. "Are the other two just as pretty as the three I have met?"

"In features." Darcy was not certain they came close to being as beautiful in character as their three older sisters were. Miss Lydia and Miss Kitty had been rather giggly and prone to fluttering lashes.

"What is your grievance with them?"

"They are too young, and I do not mean in age, though they are young in that way as well."

"Ah, so they are not candidates for friends for Georgiana?"

"Not close friends. I think she would find them too silly." She might not have six months ago, but since her ordeal with Wickham, she had changed. "However, I would not forbid her from being their acquaintance."

Young ladies often grew out of being silly, or so his aunt, Lady Matlock, had assured him when Georgiana had turned thirteen. With any amount of good fortune, the two youngest Miss Bennets would find their way to the other side of immaturity without the help of a cad.

"I would not mind her being friends with the two eldest Miss Bennets or Miss Lucas," Richard said.

"Why should she not be friends with Miss Mary?"

Richard shrugged. "I am not saying she should not be friends with Miss Mary. I just have not yet decided if I approve of her or not. She is very direct and disagreeable."

Darcy chuckled. "Yes, having friends or relations who are direct and disagreeable is a burden." He gave Richard a pointed look to taunt him.

"I am not disagreeable," Richard grumbled.

"I think both Miss Elizabeth and Miss Mary would argue with that."

"I apologized."

He had. In fact, Richard had not been unaffected by Miss Elizabeth's hasty departure from this very room two days ago. Had he not been so invested in conducting his meeting and tea with Mrs. Bennet, he might have chased after her to see that she was well.

"That is the trouble with directness," Richard muttered to himself.

"Indeed," Darcy agreed as he applied himself to the journal on his lap and began reading silently.

There was a near tragedy in the area today. The book in which Mrs. Nichols keeps her list of things to do and purchase went missing on a return trip from Meryton. She had gone to town to order the things needed for dinner when Darcy visits on his return from Rosings.

God bless him for his diligence in attending Lady Catherine. That woman is as pleasant as brandy poured on an open wound! I do not know how Darcy manages to tolerate her and her insistence that he marry her daughter. If he must have a trying mother-in-law, he should at least get a more interesting and robust wife than his poor cousin in the exchange. Miss de Bourgh is a lovely young thing despite her weak constitution and her mother. But these are not things I have not written before. Allow me to return to the near tragedy.

Mrs. Nichols was beside herself when she realized that her book was missing. She searched the cart and every parcel thoroughly and was just about to order Sam to drive her back to Meryton so she could search there when a blessed angel arrived bearing the precious book.

Miss Elizabeth, along with her sisters and mother, had been to visit their Aunt Philips and were returning home when she saw the book lying beside the lane. Mrs. Bennet had wanted to send it with a footman from Longbourn to Netherfield, but Miss Elizabeth assured her mother she could do it more quickly. According to Miss Elizabeth, it did not take too much convincing for Mrs. Bennet to allow her to do as she wished. It had only taken the mention of what a panic the missing book must be causing.

Mrs. Bennet is no scholar, and she might indulge her children more than she should, but it is not because she does not have a good heart. She feels quite deeply for the concerns of others. Perhaps too intensely, but that is why there are morning calls for sharing concerns and salts for when it all becomes too vexing, would you not agree? I tease, though only somewhat. My neighbors are not without fault, but they are good neighbours.

Mrs. Nichols was overjoyed to receive her book and sent Miss Elizabeth home with a cake for her mother. She also insisted that Sam drive Miss Elizabeth home. Miss Elizabeth protested it, as one might expect her to do. She does not like to put people out unnecessarily. However, it was no hardship for Sam since, like several other young men in the area, he is enamoured with her. Ah, she is special. I do hope, when the time comes for her to leave us and create her own life elsewhere, that she finds a good husband – one with a healthy fortune, a good heart, and a kind disposition.

Darcy could not agree more with Mr. Enfield. Miss Elizabeth was special and deserved a worthy husband.

"Do you still have that list of gentlemen who we invited?" he asked Richard, who nodded.

"Why?"

"I just wanted to see which of them we should first recommend to Miss Elizabeth." That is if there were any there who was truly worthy of her. The more Darcy got to know Miss Elizabeth in person and through Mr. Enfield's journals, he was not certain there was such a fellow on the list of party guests. Still, he would attempt to find one.

"I feel I owe it to Mr. Enfield to see her well-matched if I can, for, from what I have read in this journal, he most certainly loved her and wanted to see her happy." And strangely, though he had only known Miss Elizabeth for a few days, seeing her happy was quickly becoming one of Darcy's greatest desires.

Chapter 8

SEPTEMBER 18, 1811

"I added these rosettes to the band just here," Elizabeth indicated the three small yellow roses near where the ribbon used to secure her hat to her head attached to the bonnet. "There was just enough ribbon left from trimming a dress to make these."

"And will you wear the dress with this hat?" Miss Darcy asked.

"Oh, certainly! This is one of my favourite bonnets so it will get worn with most of my dresses at some point."

"I can see why you like it. The style is very simple – not that I mean it is simplistic or unrefined. It is just not ornate." Miss Darcy seemed to stumble over the words of her explanation as if worried that she might offend. There was such a quiet, gentleness about Miss

Darcy's character that was endearing and called to Elizabeth to nurture. This blossoming friendship with Miss Darcy was one of the things she would cherish about being required to prepare for and attend the colonel's house party.

"I think simple is the perfect word," Elizabeth assured her. "I do like decorations and embellishments, but I wish for them to be reserved and not garish." Like the large bloom sprouting from Miss Bingley's hat.

"That sounds almost precisely like what I prefer," Miss Darcy said. "However, I am very fond of flounces, and you do not appear to favour them."

"A few are tolerable, but I am afraid I am not very flouncy. Be that as it may, I do very much like the ruffles on your dress. They are just perfectly placed and not too large to be a hindrance when participating in an activity such as we are." Elizabeth looked to where Jane was lifting her bow and Mr. Bingley was instructing her on how best to shoot her arrow. "I am delighted to have been asked to join you today, and I know my sisters were also happy to be included in your fun."

Colonel Fitzwilliam had thought it was an excellent idea that they gather for some shooting practice so that he could be assured that Elizabeth was prepared for the party. He had presented the idea more gently than that, but that was, in essence, what he had said. Ever since that day when they had created the list of people to invite, he had been attempting to make amends for his remarks about the party being a *Marry Miss Elizabeth* party, but his success seemed doomed to be hindered by his forthright nature.

"You cannot be any happier than I am." Miss Darcy leaned toward Elizabeth and lowered her voice. "Do you think your sister could like Mr. Bingley?"

"I am certain she could. In fact, I am quite certain any lady could like him. He is very agreeable and handsome." She watched a shadow of question furrow Miss Darcy's brow before she spoke.

"That is not what I meant," she whispered.

"Forgive me. I was teasing."

"Oh! You do it very well! You seemed so serious in your response that I was certain that either I had not asked the right question, or you had not understood me."

She was smiling. Therefore, Elizabeth assumed she was not offended by the jesting.

"To answer what you were asking, I believe it would take very little persuasion from Mr. Bingley for Jane to lose her heart completely." And that worried Elizabeth, for she had yet to discover what sort of man Mr. Bingley was. "He is not the sort to play with a lady's heart, is he?" Miss Darcy was, most likely, the best source from whom to discover what Elizabeth needed to know.

"No, never," Miss Darcy hurried to assure her. "He is far too honorable to treat someone so shabbily as that. My brother would not keep him as a friend if he were."

There was no small amount of love shared between Miss Darcy and her brother. From all that Elizabeth had seen in the past week and a half when they had met in church or in a drawing room at either Longbourn or Netherfield, Miss Darcy adored her brother, and he doted on her. It was charming to watch the two.

"Miss Mary, it is your turn to show us what you can do," Colonel Fitzwilliam called as he crossed the lawn to collect arrows.

He had been running between shooter and target all morning, and he appeared to be revelling in the activity.

"Bingley will show you how to stand."

"I already know how to stand, Colonel," Mary retorted. She was still not fond of the colonel. Her temper did not readily yield once it was roused, and the colonel's insistence on a house party had riled it.

"I can see that you do," he admitted when he had returned from gathering arrows and was presenting them to her.

She accepted an arrow with a *thank you* and then, lifting her bow, placed the arrow and drew back. The arrow flew straight and true to the target where it lodged itself firmly between two outer rings.

"If you shift gaze to your right –" The colonel stopped speaking when she lowered her bow and glared at him.

"Are you saying that it only counts as a good hit if it kills the target instead of wounding it?" she asked.

"That is the objective."

"Perhaps it is for you, but it may not be for me." She lifted her bow and arrow again. This time, the arrow found its way to a place between the outer rings directly across from her first arrow.

The colonel chuckled. "I think it is just that you cannot hit the center," he taunted.

"Maybe," she said with a smile. "Or maybe, I find more joy in vexing you than in hitting the center." She then drew her bow back and let her arrow fly straight to the center of the target.

"Lizzy, it is your turn." She held out the bow in Elizabeth's direction and gave the colonel a smug smile.

"She could have put them all in the center, and not just that one. She has always been better than the rest of us at shooting, throwing, and playing billiards," Elizabeth said to Miss Darcy who giggled.

"Miss Elizabeth." Mr. Darcy had claimed the bow from Mary and stood waiting to give it to her. "Do you need instruction?"

"Allow me to shoot the first arrow, and then, you can tell me how to improve." She knew how to shoot, but her shots were not terribly accurate. She pulled the string with the arrow back. A finger lifted her elbow, drawing her attention.

Mr. Darcy smiled and removed his finger from her elbow. "There is no need to waste an arrow if I can see an error from the start, is there?"

"No, I am sure there is not." Especially since his touch had made that elbow tingle in the most delightful way.

"Your form is good other than the dropped elbow."

And yet, her arrow did not hit the mark, instead, it hit the target on the edge and bounced off.

"A slight shift." Mr. Darcy stepped close to her as she readied herself to shoot her second arrow and gently positioned her arms and turned her shoulders. "Now," he said close to her ear, "fix your eyes on where you want the arrow to hit."

Elizabeth drew two steadying breaths before releasing the arrow. Not because she needed them to build up the courage to shoot or some such thing. No, it was not the arrow or the target which caused her to need a moment. It was that Mr. Darcy's presence was rather disquieting in a pleasant sort of fashion, and as it turned out, his instruction was good, for this time Elizabeth's arrow found a place to stick in the target between two inner rings.

"Well done!" Mr. Darcy handed her the third arrow.

She lifted her bow, positioned the arrow, and purposefully, did not square her shoulders.

"Almost perfect." Mr. Darcy once again stepped close to her, causing her heartbeat to quicken. It was a most unusual sensation.

Charlotte's brothers had helped Elizabeth with things like this before, but their closeness had never made her heart race or caused warmth to spread throughout her body. There was something different about Mr. Darcy. She hoped it was not just because he was more handsome than Charlotte's brothers, for if that were all it was, then, she would feel very foolish and wanton.

"Excellent," he said from where he still stood behind her when her arrow once again hit the target and stuck. "I dare say that next time you will be able to perform just as well without my assistance."

That was a pity.

"Thank you," she said. "I hope that I will remember how to hold my shoulders when we get to this activity at the house party."

"Asking a gentleman for assistance might actually help you catch his attention," the colonel said.

"I will remember that should any gentleman, who is in attendance, happen to be one whom I wish to snare, Colonel."

"We have been looking at the list," Mr. Darcy said as Miss Bingley came to claim the bow and wait for the colonel to return with her arrows.

"Mr. Darcy," she said, "I am not certain I know how to do this."

"I have seen you shoot arrows before," Darcy replied. "You know what you are doing."

So did Elizabeth, and it had nothing to do with shooting arrows.

"But I might not remember," she added with a pout.

"Richard can help you."

"But I prefer you."

Oh, that was not hard to see. Miss Bingley had been doing her best to keep close to Mr. Darcy all day.

"I need to speak to Miss Elizabeth about potential suitors."

Miss Bingley cast an accusatory look in Elizabeth's direction, but then she smiled and said, far too sweetly, "How kind of you to be so helpful in finding Miss Elizabeth a husband."

"I do not need help," Elizabeth said to Mr. Darcy as she placed her hand on his proffered arm.

"While I am certain you do not require help and are quite capable of making your own decisions, I did go through the list several times and have arrived at a list of three gentlemen who seem to fit what Mr. Enfield wished for you to find in a husband." He led her away from the others as he spoke.

"What do you mean *what Mr. Enfield wished for me to find in a husband*? How do you know what he wanted for me?"

"Do not be distressed. I have only just discovered his thoughts in the journals he left to me."

"He wrote about me in his journals?" What a shocking thing to discover! She hoped he had written good things.

Mr. Darcy's head bobbed up and down. "You are featured in his thoughts often. He seems to think of you as the daughter he never had."

"Truly?" That sounded as if what was written about her was commendable.

"Yes." Darcy stopped at the edge of the lawn before it gave way to paths. "You did not know?"

"No. I mean, I knew he doted on me, but I never expected he would write about me in his journals." Nor would she have thought that he would consider who she should marry.

"Whether you expected it or not, it was done."

Elizabeth shook her head. It was odd to think of Mr. Enfield sitting at his desk and telling a blank page about her. "What did he think I need in a husband?"

Mr. Darcy pulled a slip of paper from his pocket and handed it to her. "These are the names of the gentlemen I think would be best to consider. As you can see, Mr. Harrison and Mr. Morris meet all three requirements, but Mr. Ward is lacking somewhat in the one requirement which I thought you would value least."

On the slip of paper, the names of the three gentlemen Mr. Darcy had mentioned were all written in a column down the left edge. Across the top, Mr. Darcy had written *healthy fortune, good heart, kind disposition*. And under those headings, he had placed a tick mark for the name of each gentleman if they met the criteria. There were also notes next to the marks.

Mr. Ward was the only one not to have a mark under the heading about fortune. Instead, he had a note that his income was only about two thousand a year. She smiled first because two thousand a year was a more than ample fortune, and then, because Mr. Darcy had realized that she valued a gentleman's character above his bank account.

"I happen to know that Mr. Morris is actively involved with several charities," Mr. Darcy said. "While others of his class and age are wasting money on foolish bets and frivolities, he is using his money to help the less fortunate. Added to that, I have never heard so much as a whisper about a disgruntled servant in his employ.

"Mr. Harrison cares for his mother. She is a wonderful woman. I think that you would like her and that she would like you. I base that assumption on the fact that she reminds me in a lot of ways of Mr. Enfield. Mr. Harrison also has two younger brothers in his care. Neither has finished university."

"And Mr. Ward, what makes him rank so highly in your opinion?" Elizabeth asked. His character must be exceptional if it was enough for Mr. Darcy to recommend him without a large fortune.

"Mr. Ward was raised by his grandfather who was the first in his family to be a landed gentleman. Old Mr. Ward believed in hard work and a humble disposition. His grandson has learned that well. There are those who would torment a fellow such as Mr. Bingley because his wealth came from trade, but not Mr. Ward. He went out of his way to befriend those whom others looked down on in school."

"You have known him for some time then?"

Mr. Darcy nodded. "I have."

Elizabeth studied the form of the letters that made up the names and details on the paper she held. The figures were meticulously drawn. Their creator seemed to be an excessively careful gentleman.

"I have not offended you with my list, have I?" Mr. Darcy asked.

"How can I be offended by such careful consideration of my happiness?" Truly, how could she be? It was extraordinary that Mr. Darcy had put himself out so much on her behalf as to create this thoughtful list.

"You may be offended by the very fact that I was presuming to know what would make you happy."

Elizabeth chuckled. "I was not looking for an answer, Mr. Darcy." But it was a good one.

"My apologies," he said.

"No, no, you have no need to apologize. I assume you thought of how I might be offended before you approached me with this list, and I am grateful for that."

"I did consider it. I made that list several days ago, but I could not bring myself to present it to you until today.

He was not only careful in what he did; he was also anxiously concerned about her feelings. Between those facts and the way he cared for his sister, his name should be on this list and, most likely, it should sit at the top. However, she knew he was not looking for a wife, and if he were to be looking for one, it would not be her. Why else would he be trying to find her a husband amongst his acquaintances? That was rather too bad.

"If any of these gentlemen are as considerate and compassionate as you are, Mr. Darcy, then, I think I just may find a gentleman to my liking at this party. Whether or not they are looking for someone like me remains to be seen."

Mr. Darcy laughed. "I am certain that they will be enchanted with you."

Did he find her enchanting? Or was he just saying what was polite?

"In fact," he continued, "I dare say you will have your pick of several gentlemen at this party."

Elizabeth shook her head. "I think you give me too much credit, sir. I am not the sort of lady who has gentlemen falling at her feet."

"According to Mr. Enfield, you are."

"How could he say that?"

"He seems to think that many young men in the area have been enamoured with you."

"If they were, they kept it a secret from me, or perhaps that is why they all flock to Jane, so they can be close to me without revealing their true desire." She laughed at the preposterousness of such a thing.

"Laugh as much as you like, Miss Elizabeth, but it is either true or Mr. Enfield is a liar. You would not call him a liar, would you?"

His sly grin softened his features in such an agreeable way that it took a moment for Elizabeth to reply, but when she did, she, of course, declared that she did not think of Mr. Enfield as a liar.

"I can understand why they would be enamoured with you if they saw you the way Mr. Enfield describes," Mr. Darcy said.

"You have made me very curious about what Mr. Enfield has said, but I will not ask."

"You will not?"

She shook her head. "What is contained within a journal is private."

"Not in this case," Mr. Darcy replied. "I had thought the same when they were first given to me, but these were written to those who would read them in the future. Indeed, they are written in a style very much like how a letter to a good friend is written, and since Mr. Enfield intended for me to have them and preserve them for future generations, I am certain that he would not be offended at all if you wanted to read what he has written."

The thought was intriguing.

"What say you, Miss Elizabeth? Would you like for me to share Mr. Enfield's journals with you?"

Should she give in to her curiosity?

"I promise not to think less of you for reading them." He said it as if he were trying to coax her into doing what she wanted to do.

"You are absolutely positive that I would not be intruding on Mr. Enfield's privacy if I read them?"

"Completely."

He was not the sort of gentleman who did things flippantly. His care in creating that list of three names for her proved that.

"Very well, then, I will allow my curiosity to be satisfied."

"In that case, tomorrow," he said, "I will meet you in your garden and give you the journal that I have not yet read, and when you are done with it and I am done with the one I am currently reading, we will exchange."

"This seems wrong."

"It is not. I would never do anything to lead you astray, Miss Elizabeth. My honour would not allow it."

And as those gallant words wrapped themselves around her, Elizabeth once again felt that odd, heart-racing, warmth-producing feeling she had felt when he helped her with her bow and arrow. If only he were looking for a wife and would add his name to her list, she thought with a silent, wistful sigh.

Chapter 9

SEPTEMBER 25, 1811

A week to the day later, Darcy stood at the window in the drawing room, watching for a particular lady to walk out of the wildwood and step into her garden. He did not allow his eyes to focus too directly on the spot where he knew he would first see Miss Elizabeth for there were others in the room with him, and he could feel their eyes on him.

"It is a gloomy day. Would you not agree, Mr. Darcy?" Louisa asked.

"There are a few clouds," he replied. The day was grey, but it held the promise of spending a few minutes in the garden with Miss Elizabeth. Therefore, it could not be classified as gloomy.

"It might rain," Caroline said.

"It might," he agreed.

"It would not do to get caught out in the rain," Louisa added. Apparently, Mrs. Hurst had deciphered that he would not be staying indoors with her and her sister all afternoon.

"It depends on the sort of rain it is." Richard came to stand next to Darcy. "Wet stockings would be more enjoyable than being held captive in this drawing room," he grumbled in a whisper.

"What was that, Colonel?" Louisa asked.

"Nothing for your ears," he replied. "If I had not already taken a ride," he muttered. "How do you tolerate them?"

"Not well today," Darcy answered honestly.

Caroline and her sister had been in their best disagreeable form today. There was nothing to be found in their surroundings or the possibility of the guests who would begin arriving in three days that would lift them out of their sticky mire of disparagements.

"I'm sure they think they are presenting themselves as ladies of a certain station should," he whispered to Richard.

At least, that was what he was telling himself to try to make their unpleasantness tolerable. He had heard many a lady of the *ton* use criticism as a way to promote herself. It was both an unattractive habit and one which sat high on the list of attributes he did not want in a wife.

"Do all men share so many secrets?"

"No, Mrs. Hurst, they do not," Richard replied. "However, some share far more secrets than they should, much like some women do."

"Are you gossiping?" Louisa prodded.

"No, we are not. We just have things we do not wish for you to hear," Richard said.

"Are they shocking?"

"More than likely, my dear," Mr. Hurst said. "About what, other than shocking things, could Mr. Darcy and Colonel Fitzwilliam be speaking? If it were anything else, we would not be excluded."

"There are things other than those which are shocking that one might discuss in soft tones." Richard had turned from the window but had not left Darcy's side.

Darcy could feel the agitation radiating off him. If she were wise, Mrs. Hurst would tread lightly.

"Not everything shared in private is indelicate," Richard continued. "Some is just news that does not signify to those who are unconnected to the content of the discussion."

"I do not understand," Louisa said.

"He means that whatever he and Darcy are discussing is none of your business," Bingley said.

Bingley was starting to look a trifle frazzled. He was the sort of fellow who needed to do more than sit for hours in a drawing room.

"Are you calling at Longbourn today?" Darcy asked.

Bingley's lips curled into a smile. "I wish I were, but no. Are you?"

"Why would I?"

"You seem partial to Miss Elizabeth," Mr. Hurst replied.

"I suppose I am. She and Georgiana have become friends, and Richard and I are helping her find a husband."

"At the house party or before?" Caroline's tone and look were both cutting.

"Jealous?" Richard taunted.

Bingley chuckled.

Darcy's ears burned. It was not the first time he had heard the veiled comments of the ladies in the room that he was more than merely Miss Elizabeth's friend. However, that is all he was.

"I wonder what your mother will think of her," Caroline said to Richard, who shrugged.

"It can be no less than what she thinks of you," he replied, causing Caroline to gasp.

"Lady Matlock has always treated my sister well," Louisa protested.

"That is my point exactly. My mother is a credit to her title, for her disposition is universally welcoming, gracious, and kind."

"Indeed, she is all those things," Darcy agreed quickly. There was an edge to Richard's tone that foretold of danger should Caroline continue this path of discussion.

"I do not disagree that Lady Matlock is all that is good, but even the best lady has her limits of what is and what is not acceptable."

Darcy groaned silently. Neither of Bingley's sisters seemed particularly gifted with intelligence today.

"Surely," Caroline continued, "she would not condone a match between someone from the upper circles of society and a lady as lowly as Miss Elizabeth. I am surprised she is even willing to oversee your house party."

Richard folded his arms across his chest and glared at Caroline. There were many things one could speak poorly about in front of Richard, and he would laugh and brush them aside. However, his mother was never in that number. There were few gentlemen who so openly adored their mothers as Richard did.

"If you think my mother could not tolerate myself or Darcy marrying Miss Elizabeth, who, I will remind you, is a gentleman's daughter, then your hope of ever snaring Darcy is truly non-existent. Not that you have a hope as it is. *I* would oppose a union between him and someone as disagreeable as you. My mother would allow it if it made Darcy happy. Not that you could ever make him happy."

Caroline's cheeks were flaming red, and her nostrils flared as she breathed. To say she was livid would be stating the facts lightly.

Richard glanced at Bingley. "I will be in the garden if you wish to speak to me about my cutting remarks. Bring whatever weapon you choose, for I will not withdraw what I have said."

He grabbed Darcy's arm. "You and Georgiana are coming with me. I think we need to discuss the influence of some acquaintances upon our charge."

"Come now, Colonel," Hurst protested. "One cannot fault Caroline for saying what all of society would think."

"One can, and one did," Richard replied.

"I am happy to know that your mother is better than all others." Louisa's tone was caustic.

"Stop talking," Bingley bellowed. "Good heavens, Louisa! You and Caroline have become the most annoying harpies."

"Now just a minute!" Hurst cried.

"Do you truly want to be cut off from Darcy and his family?"

Hurst looked cautiously at Darcy and Richard.

"You do not," Bingley answered his own question on Hurst's behalf, "for then, you will also be cut off from me and will have Caroline as your sole responsibility. I do not plan to give up my friend."

"You would let them," Louisa waved a hand toward Richard and Darcy, "speak so harshly about Caroline?"

"It was not *them*. It was Richard, and yes, I would. You know what I have told you about a possible match between Darcy and Caroline."

"But a gentleman can be worked on," Louisa cajoled.

"Not by speaking poorly of his aunt or the friend of his sister." Bingley stood. "It might be best if you did not stay for the party."

"I am not leaving," Caroline protested.

"If you want her to find a husband..." Louisa let the thought hang in the air.

"I suggest we let things settle before any decisions are made." Darcy regretted the words before he had even finished uttering them because of the way Louisa's expression took on an air of hope and delight.

"Miss Bingley did add some names to the list of gentlemen who we invited. Perhaps one of them will want her," Richard said. "Not that I know why they would," he muttered under his breath.

"Are you certain you wish to have her present?" Bingley asked.

Richard pressed his lips together and shook his head. "Let her stay," he said in opposition to what his body language expressed. "But I will not have her even hinting at a flaw in my mother, Miss Elizabeth, or Miss Elizabeth's sisters if she does."

"But the Bennets are wanting," Hurst protested.

Richard's eyes narrowed, and he took a step toward Hurst, who threw his hands up defensively.

"Very well, if you want to introduce such people to Lady Matlock," he said.

Richard drew a deep breath and exhaled it in a low growling tone. However, he said not a word, choosing rather to pull Darcy from the room with him.

"Georgiana, get your hat!" he barked from the corridor.

"Go outside." Darcy gave Richard a push toward the door. "I will wait for Georgie, who, I will have you know, does not care for Caroline any more than you or I do."

Richard's left eyebrow arched.

"Truly," Darcy assured him. "I only just discovered that since Wickham."

Another exhaled growl rumbled from Richard.

"Go outside."

"She is here," Bingley said as he joined Darcy and Richard in the entrance hall.

"Who is here?" Richard asked.

"Miss Elizabeth," Bingley said with a grin. "Darcy has been watching for her."

"Has he?" Richard said with some interest.

"My sister's jealousy is not unfounded," Bingley said as he nodded. "Not that I am attempting to excuse her behaviour," he added quickly.

"Miss Elizabeth and I have been discussing Mr. Enfield's journals," Darcy explained.

"She knows about them?" Richard gave Georgiana a hug when she joined them. "I am not angry with you. You know that, do you not?"

"Yes, of course, I do," she answered.

Then, Richard turned back to Darcy with an expectant look.

"I shared one volume with Miss Elizabeth." Darcy moved toward the door. "I figured that since she was mentioned in them, she might like to know what was written about her."

And it had been an excellent reason for her to visit her garden. He had truly been distressed by her comment about having wished she had never seen it. So distressed that he felt compelled to make her love the garden again. If only she could keep it no matter what he chose to do with Netherfield.

He smiled when he saw her pacing on the far side of the hedges that lined the square walkway, forming the border of her garden.

"That book you have been reading, is it one of Mr. Enfield's journals?" Bingley followed them out of the house.

"Yes, and I can share it with you after Miss Elizabeth has had a chance to read it. It would do you good to understand some of the neighbourhood in which you are hoping to find your home."

It was a reality that caused Darcy to once again regret that Miss Elizabeth would have to be parted from her garden. Maybe he should keep Netherfield.

Of course, when she married – and she would one day marry, she was too beautiful and charming to be a spinster – she would likely be parted from her garden whether Darcy sold Netherfield or not. None of the men on the list he had given her a week ago lived near Netherfield. What would any of them or even Miss Elizabeth, for that matter, want with a piece of land so far from their home?

He supposed she could visit her garden when she returned home to visit her parents, but who would keep it looking as lovely as it did now? Him? Would he be willing to tend to her garden on her behalf? Perhaps Georgiana could see to it since she and Miss Elizabeth were becoming such good friends.

Bingley elbowed Darcy's upper arm.

"I said I would like that," Bingley said.

"Like what?" Darcy asked.

Bingley's brow furrowed. "I would like to read the journal when Miss Elizabeth has finished reading it. Are you well?"

"Perfectly. Why?"

"It is not like you to lose the thread of a conversation. You said you thought I should read the journals. Then, I said that I would like that – three times – before you even heard me."

"I apologize." Darcy's neck felt warm, and that heat was creeping upwards toward his cheeks and ears. It was not like him to be caught woolgathering. "I was just thinking," he said by way of explanation.

"About what?" Bingley asked.

Darcy shook his head as if what he had been thinking about was of little importance. "About the fact that Miss Elizabeth will have to sell her garden."

"I can find another estate," Bingley offered. "Though it will be hard to find one to rival how much I like Netherfield, I am sure it is not impossible."

"I believe you are correct." Netherfield would be hard to match. There was something captivating about this small estate.

Darcy had always felt that Netherfield was welcoming. However, now that he had spent more than two weeks in a row here, he was beginning to feel that Netherfield itself was a part of the fabric of his family. The idea of selling it to Bingley was not off-putting, but the idea of someone wholly unrelated to him becoming master of Netherfield was a thought that Darcy could not contemplate with as much equanimity now as he could when he had first inherited Netherfield.

"I would rather have you here than anyone else," Darcy told Bingley as he stepped through the opening in the hedge and into Elizabeth's Garden.

"I see we are a large party today," Miss Elizabeth greeted him.

"You do not mind, do you?" If he were to answer that question honestly for himself, he would say he did mind. Georgiana had accompanied him here many times to visit with Miss Elizabeth, so her presence was not a problem. It was the addition of Bingley and Richard that was the issue.

"No, of course not," she replied. "I fear we will not have long to talk anyway. The clouds are heavy. In fact, my mother did not want me to take a walk for fear I would get wet and become ill. However, I had said I would be here."

"You did not have to come if you did not want to."

"That is not what I said, sir." She motioned to the benches in the garden. "Welcome to my garden. Please be seated. I cannot offer tea, but I can offer good conversation."

She sat down next to Georgiana who was on Darcy's right side, and he heard her whisper, "I was afraid it would rain before I got to see you." Her eyes lifted from his sister to him.

Was she including him in whom she had been eager to see? That was strangely pleasing and seemed to lift the grey clouds overhead.

"I did not bring the journal today because I did not want to risk it getting ruined if I got caught in the rain."

Darcy held his hands out, palms up. "As you can see, I have not brought mine either. What have you read about since we last spoke? Anything of interest?"

"I read an entertaining anecdote about a visit by Lady Catherine and her daughter." Her eyes danced with merriment. "It seems Mr. Enfield did not hold your aunt in high esteem."

Richard laughed. "No one with sense does."

"Then, may I safely assume that you will not be offended that I had a bit of a giggle at Mr. Enfield's comparison of her to Mr. Clark's mule?"

"He did not compare Aunt Catherine to a mule, did he?" Georgiana pressed her fingers against her lips to cover a giggle of her own.

Darcy loved the way his sister was so at ease with Miss Elizabeth. Theirs was a good friendship. He lifted his gaze from his sister to her friend's twinkling eyes and laughing smile.

"I am afraid he did."

"It seems fitting," Richard said.

"What did he say about our cousin?" Every time Darcy had read anything that mentioned Lady Catherine or Anne, it had also mentioned how he and she were not well suited for each other.

"He said she is as quiet as a dormouse and just as nervous."

"She is," Darcy agreed. Poor Anne had a weak constitution to begin with and then, once you added her mother's demanding nature to the situation, there was no other way for Anne to be other than quiet and anxious.

"And apparently, you and she should not get married." Elizabeth's eyes met his. Their sparkle had faded and been replaced by curiosity.

"I have no plans to marry Anne, and I never have," Darcy said with no little amount of resolve. Why did he feel that it was of such great importance that Miss Elizabeth believed him?

"But our aunt does," Georgiana said. "She thinks Fitzwilliam would be just the kind of husband Anne needs."

"I am sure he would be," Elizabeth said. "For, from what I have seen, he is very caring."

"That is not why Aunt Catherine thinks he would make a good husband for Anne," Georgiana said. "It is because he is rich, and his uncle is an earl."

"Is not Miss de Bourgh's uncle also an earl? You do share an uncle, do you not?" Elizabeth asked incredulously.

Darcy sighed. "Yes, Lord Matlock is an uncle to Anne, as well as my sister and I, which makes it seem redundant as a reason for making a match. However, it is a connection Lady Catherine does not wish to have lost by a poor match between her daughter and a gentleman of little standing."

"I see." There was still a small crease of bewilderment between Elizabeth's eyes.

"Wealth and connections," Darcy said with another sigh. "They are of great importance to Lady Catherine." They were all some ladies looked for when trying to find a husband.

That was why Caroline worked so hard to try to capture him. She was far more enamoured with his wealth and connections than she was with his person. She tried to engage him in conversations, but she lacked knowledge about most of the things he found interesting. Indeed, he had only ever found one lady with whom he could have long and captivating conversations, and that lady was currently sitting next to his sister.

Chapter 10

September 29, 1811

Elizabeth felt positively sick to her stomach, and it had nothing to do with the fact that she had not gotten home before the rain began on Wednesday after visiting her garden and the Darcys. She had not gotten so much as a sniffle from that.

Her current state of feeling unwell was completely due to the fact that there was a new gentleman sitting next to Mr. Bingley in church – one Mr. Ward, if Lady Lucas was to be believed, and there was no reason not to believe her. She was always first among the ladies to know who was who and what was what. It came from having a husband who was as interested in the comings and goings of Meryton as much as she herself was. What Lady Lucas did not know, Sir William did.

"He looks quite proper," Elizabeth's mother whispered loudly.

He was. Mr. Darcy had told her all he knew about Mr. Ward, and Elizabeth had come to the very same conclusion her mother had just now. Mr. Ward was all that was proper and likely the best choice out of all of the gentlemen who would be arriving for the house party for her to consider as a possible husband. She would keep the other two suggestions Mr. Darcy had listed in mind, but Mr. Ward would be the first gentleman whom she would try to get to know. Deciding on Mr. Ward as her first choice had been much easier when he was just a name on a piece of paper than it was now when he embodied the reality of the impending house party and its purpose.

"Perhaps, Mary…" her mother muttered.

"Lizzy needs a husband before I do," Mary whispered as she gave Elizabeth an apologetic look. Mary was still not happy about the fact that Elizabeth was being pushed to marry just so Mr. Darcy could sell his estate, but she was even less happy that their mother had been instructing her daily on how to snare a husband.

"Mrs. Bennet," Mr. Bennet whispered in a tone of warning and gave a nod toward the parson. He winked at Elizabeth and smiled.

If her nerves were not attempting to dance a reel and a cotillion in opposite directions in her stomach, Elizabeth might have been able to feel the support given to her in that small expression from her father. But as it was, she could only acknowledge that he was trying to help her feel more assured that all would be well, for she most definitely did not feel it.

Normally, Elizabeth enjoyed the Sunday service. However, today, the sermon was interminably long. The church was too warm. Her dress was uncomfortable, and her nose insisted upon itching for no reason whatsoever.

Why had Mr. Ward arrived early? Why could he not do as everyone else and wait to arrive until tomorrow? Then, she could have had one more day before facing any introductions. She dreaded having her mother present at Netherfield during those introductions, but here at church, she would not only have her mother present but also her aunt, Lady Lucas, Mrs. Long, and a host of other ladies pressing around with interest.

The house party had been the topic of conversation in every sitting room in Meryton for the past three weeks. Those who had been invited to the party were excited to meet the other gentlemen and ladies who would be in attendance, and those who had not been invited were hopeful that a possible match might be found at the next assembly in Meryton as that was the ball which would end Mr. Bingley's party.

Of course, no one was as excited as Elizabeth's mother. The fact that Mr. Bingley seemed to only have eyes for Jane had not escaped her notice, nor had Mr. Darcy's attention to Elizabeth. No amount of protest about how Mr. Darcy was just helping Elizabeth learn about the gentlemen who would be in attendance was going to move Mrs. Bennet from her belief that Mr. Darcy and his fortune were meant for Elizabeth. But it was not. Mr. Darcy had not once suggested that his name be added to the list he had given her, and, in truth, he had not shown any greater fondness for her than he did his sister.

Finally, the last *amen* was said and the service was over. What had happened between Mr. Bingley walking in with his guest and this moment, Elizabeth would not be able to say. Her attention had not been on the parson or his message, and her mind had not followed the prayers or scripture reading. Instead, she had been completely consumed with thoughts of what awaited her both now, as her mother tried to hurry her out of the pew, and tomorrow, when her mother would first, meet Lady Matlock and then, a group of unmarried men of wealth.

There was nothing to be done but for Elizabeth to summon up her courage and press forward. She could no more keep one day from turning into the next than she could wish Mr. Ward away from Meryton.

"Good day, Mr. Bingley," Mrs. Bennet said as she finally reached him.

As expected, Lady Lucas and Mrs. Long were already there. Elizabeth was certain that Aunt Phillips would be along shortly.

"Good day, Mrs. Bennet," Mr. Bingley replied before his eyes wandered to Jane and he smiled.

That smile put some of Elizabeth's anxiety to rest as it reminded her of her true purpose in subjecting herself to the matchmaking plans of Colonel Fitzwilliam. Jane and Mr. Bingley were destined for one another, and she would do her part to make certain they were allowed the chance to form a stout love that would lead to marriage.

"I see you have guests arriving already," Mrs. Bennet added when Mr. Bingley did not immediately introduce Mr. Ward.

Colonel Fitzwilliam chuckled. Mrs. Bennet did not notice it, but Elizabeth did – and so did Mary who scowled at the poor man. It was Mary's favoured expression when it came to the colonel.

"Yes, our first guest arrived late last night, and we expect the Countess to arrive before dinner."

"Oh, my!" Mrs. Bennet cried. "How exciting for you."

"We are quite delighted." Mr. Bingley motioned to Mr. Ward. "Would you allow me to introduce our first guest to you?"

"Of course."

Again, the colonel chuckled, and Mary scowled at him. Elizabeth knocked her sister's arm with her elbow.

"What?" Mary whispered.

"This is *him*," Elizabeth answered with a pointed look.

"Him? Top of the list him?"

Elizabeth nodded. She, Mary, and Jane had discussed at length all the information that Mr. Darcy had been able to share about the three men on the list he had given her. Jane had readily agreed that Mr. Ward sounded as if he was the most promising of the three options. Mary had reluctantly allowed it to be true.

"I thought that was Mr. Morris."

Elizabeth shook her head and then curtseyed as her name was listed in the those being introduced.

"Miss Bennet, Miss Elizabeth, and Miss Mary will be joining us at Netherfield on the morrow," Mr. Bingley said. "Miss Elizabeth actually owns a piece of Netherfield," he added. "Mr. Enfield left her a portion of the garden."

"Indeed? That was very kind of him. Is it a lovely portion?" Mr. Ward asked her.

"I find it quite to my liking, which is why Mr. Enfield gave it to me," Elizabeth replied.

"It is an exceptional piece of land," the colonel inserted, "but it pales in beauty to its owner."

What was he doing? Elizabeth cast a pleading look toward Mr. Darcy who was watching her closely.

"Is that so?" Mr. Ward said.

"I would not say so," Elizabeth answered. "But I thank the colonel for his compliment."

Colonel Fitzwilliam stepped forward and took a place next to Mr. Ward. "Miss Elizabeth is too modest. Even Darcy would agree that there is no flower, blooming or having already bloomed, in Netherfield's garden that is as pretty as Miss Elizabeth. What say you, Darcy?"

"There is only one answer to that, sir," Mr. Bennet said with a laugh. "The truthfulness of the reply will have to be vouchsafed by Mr. Ward after he has gained an acquaintance with both the garden and my daughter."

He extended his hand to Mr. Ward. "I am her father," he said by way of introduction. "I apologize for not being here to greet you with my wife, but Sir William had to speak to me about an estate matter. However, now that I am here, I will caution you as I would caution any other gentleman who might find himself enamoured with my daughters, handsomeness must be more than fine features."

"I could not agree with you more, Mr. Bennet," Mr. Ward said.

"Good. Your answer puts you in the way of gaining my approval."

"I am happy to hear it," Mr. Ward said.

Elizabeth's father turned to her mother. "Come along, my dear." He offered her his arm and reluctantly she took it. "Lydia, Kitty, you will join us. It was good to meet you, Mr. Ward."

"Papa," Lydia protested.

"I will not be moved," he replied.

"But Papa," she tried again while following him.

"This is your sisters' time, not yours," he said.

"Are you walking home?" Colonel Fitzwilliam asked Elizabeth.

"We are."

"Then, we will join you." He draped an arm across Mr. Ward's shoulders.

So, the colonel was going to force Mr. Ward to spend time with her, was he? Elizabeth felt very much like scowling at him as Mary was once again doing.

"Georgie has been most eager to see you," Colonel Fitzwilliam continued, "and I would like some company."

Miss Darcy's eyes grew wide at that. The colonel was playing far too hard at his role of matchmaker.

"I am happy to see you," she said to Elizabeth. "And it is a pleasant day."

"Are you dressed for the activity?" Elizabeth asked softly.

"I now understand why Richard insisted I wear my boots," she said with a smile.

"You do not have to walk with me, but I would not be opposed to your company either," Elizabeth assured her.

"Then, it is settled," Colonel Fitzwilliam declared. "Bingley, your sisters and Hurst can take the carriage to Netherfield and Darcy's driver can go ahead of us to Longbourn."

Before the colonel could start ordering who should walk with whom, Elizabeth wrapped her arm around Georgiana's, and held her other hand out to Mary, leaving Jane to Mr. Bingley's care and the other gentlemen to themselves.

"It would be better if we gentlemen each escorted one of you. We would not want you to stumble."

"Both Lizzy and I have walked to and from Meryton for many years without stumbling, Colonel," Mary said.

"You may pick us up if we topple," Elizabeth added.

Mr. Ward laughed. "I do hope that will not be necessary."

"So do I, Mr. Ward," Elizabeth assured him as she, Mary, and Georgiana began walking.

"You seem to be a very independent lady, Miss Elizabeth," Mr. Ward said as he took a spot walking next to Mary.

"She is excessively independent," Mary said.

"I am happy to hear it," he said. "I think a lady should possess some independence of spirit."

Mary smiled and, leaning closer to Elizabeth, whispered, "I approve."

So did Elizabeth. She would never consider any gentleman who thought a lady was incapable of being independent or who tried to squash such tendencies.

"Since we are about to attend a house party, and since I see no need to dance around the fact that we are all attending with the hope of finding a match," Mr. Ward continued. "I will add that I am looking for a partner in life and not merely a hostess for my home and mother for my children. My wealth is not tied to generations of gentlemen. It is from more lowly sources, and I have been brought up to expect an honest day's work from myself and those in my employ. I would wish for a wife who feels the same and who can overlook my ties to trade."

His openness about the reason he was at this house party and his desires for the type of wife he would marry was another mark in his favour. He appeared to be, as Mr. Darcy had said, a forthright gentleman.

"Ties to trade do not bother us, Mr. Ward," Elizabeth said. "My father's family has owned Longbourn for many generations, but my mother is the daughter of a country solicitor, and I have an uncle who is a merchant in town and another who is a solicitor in Meryton."

That information made Mr. Ward's features light with delight. His eyes were strikingly blue, though they, like his brown hair, were light in shade. He stood nearly a head shorter than Mr. Darcy who was walking next to him but was equal in height to both Mr. Bingley and Colonel Fitzwilliam. His coat was well-made and lay smoothly across his shoulders which were neither wide nor narrow. There was nothing about him that was ostentatious, but there was everything about him that seemed pleasant.

Elizabeth breathed a sigh of relief. Mr. Ward might be a good option to consider in reality and not just theory. Her eyes moved past him to the gentleman next to him. Mr. Ward was no Mr. Darcy, but Mr. Darcy was not on her list – the one he had made and could have put himself on if he had chosen to do so. Maybe, Mr. Ward would prove to be even more to her liking than Mr. Darcy was, even if the Mr. Darcy about whom Mr. Enfield had written in his journals was one who would be hard to equal.

"Did you have a good trip?" Elizabeth asked just as Jane asked if Mr. Ward's trip was long.

"It was an excellent journey," Mr. Ward said. "We have had exceptional weather for this time of year. I hope it continues for us."

"I do as well," Mr. Bingley said. "It would be dreadful to be forced to be inside when there is so much more we can do when outside."

"Netherfield has a ballroom. I am certain we could hold a few dances and musicales if needed," the colonel said.

"I do like to dance," Mr. Ward said. "Do you?" He looked at Elizabeth.

"I do."

"That is excellent." His eyes lingered on her for a moment before he turned to Jane. "My estate is in Cornwall, so yes, my journey was long."

"That is a distance, is it not?" Jane said with no little amount of surprise.

"It is indeed, but I also have a house in London. It is nothing large and is not in the fashionable district, but I do have a place to live while participating in the season."

"Will you keep it once you are married?" Mary asked.

"That will depend somewhat upon my wife and our budget, but I am not opposed to keeping it."

That he would consider his wife's opinion on the matter was another point in Mr. Ward's favour.

"Do you enjoy the entertainments that can be found in town?" Elizabeth always enjoyed visiting London. There were so many things of interest to be found there such as the theatre, the numerous shops, and the parks.

"I do. I particularly enjoy the museums."

"So does Elizabeth," Mary said, earning a small jab of Elizabeth's elbow.

His love of museums was a point in the man's favour, but there was no need for him to know that.

"I have never been to the museums," Mary continued, "but Jane and Elizabeth have been. They often go to visit our aunt and uncle Gardener in Gracechurch Street."

"That is the uncle who is a merchant?" Mr. Ward asked.

Mary nodded. "Uncle Philips lives in Meryton."

"He was Mr. Enfield's solicitor," Mr. Darcy said. "And a fine one at that." The smile he gave Elizabeth warmed her heart. Would Mr. Ward's smile ever do that?

She probably should have allowed the colonel to pair them off. Then, she would have been able to walk next to Mr. Ward and see if his presence would make her heart race in that pleasant fashion that Mr. Darcy's nearness always seemed to.

Chapter 11

SEPTEMBER 30, 1811

"I present to you Mrs. Bennet, Miss Bennet, Miss Elizabeth, and Miss Mary as requested, my lady." Darcy's aunt Ada, Lady Matlock, had been adamant that she be introduced just as soon as possible to the lady who was the reason for this house party.

Thankfully, the Bennets had been true to their time and had arrived early. Other than Mr. Ward, there were no other guests to get in the way of her ladyship meeting the Bennets privately.

"It is a pleasure," Lady Matlock said. "Miss Elizabeth, is it?" She held her hand out to Elizabeth.

"Yes, my lady." Elizabeth took his aunt's hand and dipped a low curtsey.

"You are truly as lovely as my son said. I also understand my husband's cousin was fond of you. I have often heard your name in correspondence."

Elizabeth blinked, and her eyes grew wide. "You have heard about me?" A hand pressed against her chest over her heart as if overwhelmed by such an honor.

Darcy had been shocked to know that fact as well when his aunt had shared it with him shortly after her arrival.

"I have, and what I have heard has been excellent. I suspect you will have no trouble finding a gentleman to admire you."

Oh, that was true. Mr. Ward seemed quite enamoured with Miss Elizabeth from their first meeting at church yesterday. Darcy should feel good about that fact. Ward was the gentleman he had selected as the best fit for Miss Elizabeth. However, being correct was not setting well with him for some reason. Maybe if he knew that Miss Elizabeth was just as enamoured – maybe that would ease his troubled mind.

She had seemed welcoming, but she was a proper sort of lady and could have been just being polite. He had watched her yesterday quite carefully and seen no hint of preference for the gentleman over what he had witnessed in all her interactions with Bingley and Richard.

"I only hope I can find a gentleman who admires me and whom I can admire in return, my lady," Miss Elizabeth replied.

"Ah, that is the rub, is it not? Equal affections are important, but I suspect you already know that." Darcy's aunt gave Miss Elizabeth one last appraising look and then turned her attention to Miss Bennet.

"I think someone at this party may have already found a match of equal affections if she is as enamoured with our host as he is with her." Aunt Ada's look of joy was almost as bright as Miss Bennet's smile. "I think very highly of Mr. Bingley and would recommend him to any lady who seemed worthy of him. My son assures me that you are such a lady."

"I thank you, my lady." Miss Bennet lowered her eyes and blushed. "I also esteem Mr. Bingley highly."

Darcy had never seen his friend so enamoured with a lady, and the truth that Bingley had found a lady to admire and who admired him in equal measure settled it in Darcy's mind. Bingley would soon be a married man.

"Mr. Bingley is a delightful young man," Mrs. Bennet agreed. "And we are hopeful."

"I believe your hopes will be achieved with a little patience," Lady Matlock assured her. "Miss Mary, I have heard some wonderful things about you as well."

"You have?" Miss Mary's eyes were wide, and she covered her mouth as if she had misspoken.

Lady Matlock chuckled. "I have. Apparently, you know your mind and are not afraid to share it."

Miss Mary's brow furrowed. "And you consider that to be a good thing?"

"I do. Some gentlemen need wives who match them in strength of opinion – not to the point of arguing at every turn and creating misery, mind you, but to the point of a lady making her husband consider her point of view on things. Have I shocked you?"

"Yes," Mrs. Bennet answered, and she looked it. Indeed, to Darcy, she looked as if she might need a chair to keep from swooning from the surprise.

"I shock many," Lady Matlock assured her. "However, being the mother of a son who is a colonel and who was firmly in possession of a disposition to be one, even before he could say his first word, I can assure you that such gentlemen do not do well with milquetoast, biddable wives. Such a lady would be constantly scurrying to keep up with her husband's demands, and of that, I most heartily *do not* approve. Therefore, I believe there is a place for ladies with strong minds and opinions, and, if I am not mistaken, there are at least two gentlemen on our guest list who would do well with such a lady as his wife." She looked to Mrs. Bennet. "I will point them out to you."

Darcy's lips tipped up in a small grin, and he shook his head ever so slightly. His aunt Ada did fancy herself an expert at reading characters and knowing who would do well with whom.

"You do me a great honor, my lady." Mrs. Bennet was positively beaming with delight.

"I understand you have two more daughters to see wed before your duties are done. It is the least I can do to be of assistance in directing a gentleman or two towards your eldest daughters."

Feet scurried softly in the corridor, and voices from in front of the house, as well as the clip-clop of hooves on stones, filtered in through the open windows of the sitting room where Lady Matlock would receive all her guests. Quiet and solitude would be in scarce supply soon. Whether Darcy liked it or not, Netherfield was about to become filled.

"I hear a carriage on the drive," Darcy interrupted.

"Ah, yes, I should make sure I am available to greet others." His aunt smiled at him. "Would you be a dear, Fitzwilliam, and show the Bennets to their rooms?"

"Me?" That seemed odd. Darcy glanced at Mrs. Bennet and her daughters. From their raised eyebrows he was not alone in finding it an unusual request.

"Miss Bingley and Mrs. Hurst will be busy with whoever has arrived."

"What about Mrs. Nichols?" he asked.

Aunt Ada merely arched a brow, and Darcy gave her a shallow bow. He knew that look too well to protest further.

"If you would follow me, I will see if we can discover which rooms are yours." He would find Mrs. Nichols and have her see these ladies to their rooms. He did not want to know in which rooms various ladies were staying. It would make it less likely for there to be rumors if he was ignorant of the housing arrangements of any lady beyond those for his sister's, and after hearing the sniping remarks about Miss Elizabeth and himself from Bingley's sisters just this morning, caution seemed wise.

"They are next to Miss Darcy's room," his aunt said with a smile. "I think you know where that is, and their things have already been delivered to the rooms." She turned to Elizabeth. "Georgiana told me how well you get along, so I insisted that you be given a place near her since she is not yet out and will not be at every activity. Having friends to visit with when they are not otherwise entertained will be good for her. Do you not agree, Fitzwilliam?"

"That does seem reasonable." Even if it did not seem reasonable, he was not about to contradict his aunt when she asked him something with such a pointed look as the one which she currently wore. "If you will follow me," he repeated to the Bennet ladies.

"Georgiana is in her room," his aunt continued. "Let her know that Miss Elizabeth has arrived, and send my son to me."

"As you wish, my lady." Darcy bowed to his aunt as a prickle of annoyance danced up his spine. He loved her, but at times, Aunt Ada was just as demanding as the son whom she wished sent to her was.

~*~

"Miss Elizabeth!" Mr. Ward exclaimed with delight as they met him on the stairs. "It is good to see you and your sisters and mother. Mrs. Hurst said you were here, but I thought you would be in your rooms."

"They had to meet my aunt first," Darcy said as he watched Elizabeth, who shifted as if uneasy but smiled in welcome to Mr. Ward.

"Mr. Bingley and I are going to greet gentlemen in the billiards room," Mr. Ward said. "Will you join us, Darcy?"

"I will once I have done as Lady Matlock requested and have helped these ladies find their lodgings and my sister."

"Capital!"

The man in front of Darcy seemed far too happy about being at a party and in company. How did other gentlemen, meaning gentlemen who were not Darcy, manage to enjoy these sorts of ordeals? Darcy would much prefer to be in the library with a good book and two or three good friends than greeting guests and engaging in insipidly mundane conversations as gentlemen entered and exited the billiards room.

"I will not keep you from your task, but I am glad I was able to see you, Miss Elizabeth, even if it was only in passing." There was no denying the man's look of admiration. It was not veiled in the least.

"She is very glad we met you, too," Mrs. Bennet inserted. Apparently, she had not missed Mr. Ward's fondness either.

"If you see my cousin," Darcy said, "would you tell him that his mother has requested his presence?"

"Most certainly."

"Oh, he seems so very pleasant and proper," Mrs. Bennet said as they continued their trek up the stairs. "And it seems he favours you, Elizabeth."

Yes, it did seem that way, and no, Mrs. Bennet had not missed it. That should make Darcy glad, excessively glad, but it did not. That was likely due to Miss Elizabeth's apparent unease at the meeting, he reasoned.

"It would likely take very little effort on your part to draw him along."

"Mama, please." Miss Elizabeth's tone was pleading.

"It is true!"

"True or not, I do not think that Mr. Darcy wants to be part of your lecture," Miss Mary said.

She was direct, and currently, that directness was the cause of Darcy's smile. Miss Mary was absolutely correct. He did not want to be part of any lecture between a mother and a daughter where that mother, Mrs. Bennet, was instructing her daughter, Miss Elizabeth, about who would make a good husband and how to secure him.

"He will need to know some of this if he wishes to help his sister find a husband."

"He has an aunt to help him," Miss Mary retorted as they gained the landing.

"And, I suppose, he could have a wife by then, too?" There was a cajoling, questioning tone to Mrs.

Bennet's statement as she turned her eyes towards him.

"I will find a wife when I am ready to find a wife," he answered. He did not need her attempting to find him a wife at this party.

"A gentleman does not always know when he is ready," Mrs. Bennet argued.

"This gentleman does."

She tipped her head and smiled at him as if he were a misguided child. "If you say so."

Her words were ones of agreement, but her tone was one of disbelief.

"I do say so."

"When do you suppose you will be ready to take a wife?" she asked.

He shook his head. He had never considered putting a date to when he would begin searching for a bride. "I am not certain I can give you a day and month."

"What about a year? Will it be this year or next?"

"I could not say."

"Then, I believe it is as I said. Gentlemen do not always know when they are ready to take a wife." Her smile was self-satisfied, and Darcy had to admit that her statement was more well reasoned out than he had expected her capable of.

"I suppose I must admit that you are right when it is stated in such a fashion. However, I believe I will still know when the time is right." He could not take a wife until he knew that he could divide his time between his estate matters, his sister, and his wife without letting any of those things languish. He had thought he might be ready to begin his search for a wife this year until Wickham had nearly ruined Georgiana.

"Do not wait too long," Mrs. Bennet cautioned as if his happiness were a genuine concern for her. "If you do, you may find yourself regretting what you could have had."

Again, her ability to follow a logical path rather than taking a circuitous meander surprised him.

"I will do my best not to wait that long."

She smiled broadly, though there was a slight cunning look to the expression. It was the expression he expected to see from every female chaperone at this party. They were all here to do their best to secure a husband for their charges, and there was no need to hide the fact here as there might be at a soiree during the season. Everyone knew that a house party was a matchmaker's heaven.

"Mr. Ward seems like a very pleasant and proper gentleman," Mrs. Bennet said.

"So you have said," Darcy agreed.

"But you have not assured me of the truth of that fact, and I would imagine you would know him better than I do."

Darcy stopped at the door next to his sister's room. "I would not disagree with your statement. Mr. Ward is an upstanding fellow. His fortune is modest, but he does not want for the drive to improve himself and his holdings."

"Only modest, you say?"

"Yes."

The door to the room that would be occupied by the Bennets stood open, and Miss Mary had already entered and disappeared into the dressing room that connected this room with the one next to it.

Mrs. Bennet pursed her lips and tipped her head this way and that. "I suppose modest is acceptable since he is such a fine gentleman of good character. Would you not agree, Elizabeth?" she called to her daughter who had followed Miss Bennet into the room in front of which Darcy stood.

"Of course, Mama," Miss Elizabeth said with a roll of her eyes that caused Darcy to bite back a smile.

This was going to be a trying time for her, too, and he once again felt a twinge of guilt that she would have to endure this at all.

"I will inform my sister that you are here."

"Thank you," Miss Elizabeth said.

"Mama, I think the other room will work best for you and me." Miss Mary had reappeared from the dressing room.

Lovely. Now, Darcy not only knew which set of rooms Miss Elizabeth might be in, but he also knew which of the two rooms would be hers. This was not information he needed to know. So, before he could end up being privy to anything more about the arrangements in Miss Elizabeth's room, Darcy moved to his sister's room and knocked on her door.

Turning, he looked back at Miss Elizabeth's room while he waited for his sister to answer her door and wondered again if Miss Elizabeth admired Mr. Ward as much as the man seemed to admire her. Of course, he could not fault Ward for his interest. Miss Elizabeth was witty, charming, and pretty. Only a fool would not find her appealing.

The door next to him opened.

"Fitzwilliam?" Georgiana looked surprised to see him.

"Aunt Ada wanted me to inform you that the Miss Bennets have arrived and are in the room next to yours."

Happiness suffused his sister's expression at the news. "Did Aunt Ada like them?"

"From what I can tell, she did. I am certain, however, she will tell us her full opinion later."

Georgiana pulled him into her room. "Was Mrs. Bennet an issue like Miss Bingley expected?"

Miss Bingley had declared many times over the past few days that Mrs. Bennet was going to behave inappropriately in the presence of a countess. For, according to either of Bingley's sisters or Mr. Hurst, simple country folk just did not know how to behave in the higher realms of society.

"No, she was all that was proper. I think she was awestruck, to be honest, and who can blame her? I am positive it is not every day that an earl's wife asks for an audience with her."

Georgiana giggled.

"She is surprising," Darcy said.

"Mrs. Bennet is?"

"I know, I am as shocked to say it as you are to hear it, but she is not exactly what I assumed. I am not saying she is a great thinker – we know that Mr. Enfield even said that – but she is not without some capability to form a logical argument."

"Did you argue with her?"

"Only about my not being ready to find a wife."

To his surprise, Georgiana did not tease him as he expected her to. Instead, she tipped her head and looked at him hopefully.

"What?"

"I would like a sister."

"And you will have one to your liking someday."

"Could I have one exactly like Miss Elizabeth?"

Darcy's eyes grew wide. That was a rather direct and specific request! "Miss Elizabeth?" he repeated. The idea was rather surprisingly appealing.

Georgiana nodded. "I think I would be perfectly content if she were my sister."

"I think she favours Mr. Ward." Not that he had any real evidence that she did. He turned sideways and motioned to the door. This was a conversation he was not prepared to have if the wild beating of his heart were to be believed. "Miss Elizabeth is waiting for you to visit her."

"Do you want to know what I think?" his sister asked as she moved toward the door of her room.

No, he was not sure he did.

Georgiana did not wait for a reply from him. "I think Miss Elizabeth could prefer you if you would allow it." She lifted up on her toes and kissed his cheek before leaving him staring mutely after her as she quit the room.

Chapter 12

OCTOBER 1, 1811

"I wish the ball was taking place here," Miss Shaw said to Mrs. Hurst. The two ladies were stood near the piano where Miss Bingley was playing.

Elizabeth was reading not far away on a sofa. She was, in fact, close enough to the trio of ladies to hear them quite clearly, even though they spoke in hushed tones.

"The ballroom is so grand," Miss Shaw continued, "and this instrument is perfection."

"I would not expect any relation of Mr. Darcy's to possess anything of inferior quality," Miss Bingley said as she played.

"Which is perhaps why Mr. Darcy has still not fallen at your feet," Miss Shaw quipped. "You have money, my dear, but you do not have the pedigree some of us do."

"He is not worshipping you either," Mrs. Hurst retorted.

"Not yet," Miss Shaw said with a light laugh. "Oh, do not glare at me like that, Caro. You know I would never set my cap at him when I know you have. You are far too dear to me to throw you over for a dour gentleman like that. However, if Mr. Darcy were as agreeable as your brother, then, I might consider it."

Elizabeth kept her eyes on her book, but she was not reading. The discussion taking place at the piano behind her was far more interesting than poetry.

"I think you should worry more about certain local ladies than you should me," Miss Shaw hissed in a whisper. "I have heard told that there is one who seems cozy with both him and his sister."

"Miss Elizabeth."

Elizabeth's mouth fell open at the obvious tone of repugnance Mrs. Hurst had used to say her name. It was no surprise that Mrs. Hurst did not like her. Elizabeth had known that nearly from the moment they met, but it was still startling to hear the depth of distaste with which her name had been said.

"Mr. Ward adores her," Miss Bingley said as papers shuffled between songs. "We have only to ensure that a match is formed there."

Mr. Ward. Elizbeth sighed silently. He had been rather open with his admiration yesterday when they met on the stairs and had continued to be most attentive for the remainder of the day. He would be a good choice if Elizabeth could only get her heart to agree with her head. There truly was nothing off-putting about the gentleman, and what lady did not wish to be adored by a handsome man of upright character? Apparently, the answer to her question was herself. Perhaps hers was the silliest heart in all of England, or maybe it was just slow in coming to the point.

Whichever option was the truth of the matter, the fact remained that, in all the times that she and Mr. Ward had been together, her heart had not once galloped away with her or caused her to feel that wonderful warm feeling that Mr. Darcy always brought with him whenever he was near. Was she doomed to be miserable and alone with her heart forever tainted by longing for what could not be?

"I have not noted any particular regard on her part," Miss Shaw said. "She is polite but no more than friendly – unlike her sister and your brother." Miss Shaw laughed again. "I imagine you are *delighted* with that match."

"I should think we are not," Mrs. Hurst retorted. "Charles can do better than a country nobody."

"Miss Bennet would be sought after in town," Miss Shaw said. "I know she has little money to her name and no real connections, but her beauty surpasses most." Miss Shaw sighed. "And she is sweet. Those are the worst sorts of beauties for they make it dreadfully hard for me to dislike them."

"You are too soft," Mrs. Hurst said. "I thought you favoured Charles at one point?"

"I did, but…"

"But what?"

"My mother did not approve. Now, if he had owned this estate when he was showing me attention, she might have been more accepting of your father being a tradesman. It would be an excellent thing if he did purchase this estate…for your sake, Caro."

"Mr. Darcy cares little about if someone has ties to trade or not. If he did, he and Charles would not be such good friends," Miss Bingley replied.

"Having a friend with ties to trade is different than having a wife with such connections," Miss Shaw said.

"Then, if we want my brother to purchase this estate, we simply must see that Miss Elizabeth and Mr. Ward make a match," Mrs. Hurst said.

"Why?" Miss Shaw asked.

Elizabeth caught her breath. Mrs. Hurst would not tell Miss Shaw about the need for Elizabeth to marry, would she?

"So Mr. Darcy can sell this estate to Charles, of course."

She would. Elizabeth felt ill.

"I do not understand. Why does Miss Elizabeth need to make a match with Mr. Ward before Mr. Darcy can sell Netherfield."

"Because," Mrs. Hurst spoke in such a low tone that Elizabeth could barely hear her, "Miss Elizabeth inherited a portion of the garden, and the estate cannot be sold unless it is whole."

"Cannot Mr. Darcy purchase the garden from Miss Elizabeth?"

"Miss Elizabeth cannot sell it until she is married."

"Indeed?" shock suffused Miss Shaw's tone.

"She has so little by way of wealth and such regrettable familial connections that I am sure that Miss Elizabeth's inheritance was Mr. Enfield's way of helping the less fortunate."

Oh! Mrs. Hurst was the most disagreeable woman Elizabeth had ever met! *Little by way of wealth? Regrettable connections? Less fortunate*? It was not as if Elizabeth were a pauper, and she, unlike Mrs. Hurst, was a gentleman's daughter!

"Of course, we shall do our part to help her succeed with Mr. Ward because we are the charitable sort." Mrs. Hurst laughed. "That is why we have been forced to have this party after all. It is so *she* can find a husband."

Elizabeth closed her book and rose. She had heard enough. She did not need to listen to them laugh and talk about her any more than she had. She would love to turn and tell them exactly what she thought of them. However, that would not help Jane.

Mr. Bingley's sisters already did not like Jane. There was no reason to give them more of a cause to dislike her. Jane's best chance at a happy future depended upon Elizabeth clamping her tongue firmly between her teeth and leaving the room as if she had not heard a thing.

"Are you well?" Charlotte asked when she joined Elizabeth in the hall.

"No, but I will be." Eventually. After a good stomp around her room as she scolded an imaginary Miss Bingley and Mrs. Hurst.

"What happened?"

Elizabeth took Charlotte by the hand and pulled her along as she climbed the stairs towards her room.

"Mrs. Hurst told Miss Shaw that I must marry to sell my garden and that I am the reason for this party."

"She did not!"

"Shhh! Do not draw attention to us," Elizabeth hissed. She just wanted to escape to her room without the need to be polite to anyone. If she were not so determined to remain here and attempt to find a husband so that Mr. Bingley had enough time to fall irrevocably in love with Jane, Elizabeth would gather her things when she entered her room and walk home.

"What are you going to do?" Charlotte asked.

"What can I do? I was not supposed to hear that conversation. Only you and I know I have heard it. Therefore, I am going to have to go on as if nothing happened and pretend that everyone here does not know that I need help finding a husband."

"Not everyone knows," Charlotte protested.

"They will." Elizabeth tossed the door to her room open. "You know they will know before dinner is served tonight." A juicy piece of gossip such as Mrs. Hurst had shared was too tantalizing not to share.

"Who will know what by dinner?" Mary popped her head out of the dressing room door.

"Everyone will know that I am the reason for this party and that I am unable to find a husband without help and charity." Elizabeth flung herself on the bed.

"How will they know that?"

"Mrs. Hurst told Miss Shaw," Charlotte explained. "Elizabeth heard the conversation, but they do not know she heard it."

"You were eavesdropping?"

"Yes. And, before you say it, I know nothing good ever comes from listening to things that are not meant for me to hear." It was a common saying that fell from Mary's lips whenever someone began to tell a story they had overheard.

Mary sat on the edge of the bed and placed a hand on Elizabeth's left knee. "I am sorry to be right," she said softly.

Elizabeth covered her face as tears pricked her eyes. "I want to go home."

"You cannot," her younger sister said firmly. That was the thing about Mary, she could be so soft and gentle in one moment and then stern and unbending in another.

"I know I cannot, but I want to."

Elizabeth did not want to remain here and be pushed toward Mr. Ward by her mother, Colonel Fitzwilliam, Mr. Bingley's sisters, and probably anyone else Mrs. Hurst could enlist to help her in the get-Elizabeth-married project.

"They also do not think Jane is good enough for their brother," she said.

"They are idiots."

Elizabeth chuckled at Mary's words.

"She is right," Charlotte agreed. "They have it backward, for no one is good enough for Jane, I say. However, Mr. Bingley is close enough to pass. If he did not have sisters, he would be even closer to good enough, but alas, no one can choose whether or not they have sisters."

Again, Elizabeth chuckled. Both she and Charlotte had younger sisters who were challenging to love at times.

"Neither Maria nor Lydia will ever be so callous as Miss Bingley and Mrs. Hurst, will they be?" Mary asked.

"No, they will not be," Charlotte said firmly. "Because I will not allow it."

"I am not sure even you can prevent them from taking a wrong path if they decide upon taking it," Elizabeth said. Both Maria and Lydia possessed strong, determined wills.

"You, Jane, and Mary will marry well, and Kitty and Lydia will benefit from it."

"Jane and Lizzy will marry well," Mary said. "It remains to be seen if I am ever to marry."

"You will marry," Charlotte protested. "But even if you do not, you will live with Lizzy and will help your younger sisters when they visit."

"I do not want to help them." Mary folded her arms.

"Who says I am going to even marry?" Elizabeth cried.

"Mr. Ward is taken with you. I dare say he will propose before the party has concluded." Charlotte put Elizabeth's fear into words.

"I do not want him to propose," she admitted.

"Why not?" Charlotte asked. "He is perfectly lovely."

Elizabeth covered her face again. This time it was to hide her embarrassment. "He does not stir my heart."

"You can learn to love him."

Charlotte was far too practically minded.

"And, if Mr. Ward were to fancy you, would you accept him instead of Mr. Taylor?" Mary asked.

"Not unless there was no way I would ever be able to marry Mr. Taylor. However, that is not the same as Elizabeth accepting Mr. Ward without her heart being fully engaged." Her head tipped as she looked at Elizabeth. "Is it?"

Elizabeth shook her head. "No, but I still do not want to marry without equal affections."

"Then, attempt to love Mr. Ward now," Charlotte counselled. "Unless there is someone else whom you already love." She shared a look with Mary that seemed to say that they already knew that there was someone Elizabeth loved.

"You mean like Mr. Darcy," Mary said.

Elizabeth looked from Charlotte to Mary and back. "Why would you think I love Mr. Darcy?"

Both Charlotte and Mary laughed.

"I repeat. Why would you think I love Mr. Darcy?"

"We have known you long enough to know when you favour something or someone," Charlotte said, "and you favour Mr. Darcy. Your smiles for him are not the same as they are for Mr. Ward, and you watch him far more than you watch anyone else."

"He is a friend."

"Are you saying that you do not want him to ever be anything more?" Mary's expression was one that said she would not accept any answer other than the one she expected, which was, of course, the truth. Elizabeth wished with all that was in her that Mr. Darcy had put his name on that list he had made.

"He did not include himself on the list he gave me. Therefore, it matters not what I may or may not want."

"Do you truly love him?" Charlotte asked as if she were surprised by the fact. Her surprise was likely due more to the fact that Elizabeth had admitted the truth than anything else.

"I admire him." Love seemed too strong a word. It was a word that threatened to cause more pain when it was not reciprocated than not being admired in return would.

"Then make him wish he were on the list," Mary said.

"You cannot make someone love you if they do not wish to do so," Elizabeth argued.

"Do you know that he does not wish to love you? Has he told you?"

"He did not put himself on the list!" Elizabeth cried. Mary could be so frustratingly unmovable at times.

The door opened, and Mary's replying protest died on her lips until they all saw that it was just Jane who had entered.

"He might not have known to put himself on the list when he made it, and to ask for his name to be added now when you appear to be enamoured with Mr. Ward would seem like a foolish thing to do."

"I am not enamoured with Mr. Ward."

"You seem welcoming."

"Welcoming is not the same as enamoured!"

"What are you and Mary arguing about?" Jane asked.

"Whether or not Lizzy should try to make Mr. Darcy love her," Charlotte said.

"Do you like him?" Jane asked excitedly.

"She *admires* him," Mary said with a roll of her eyes.

"But he is not on the list," Elizabeth protested again. Why was it that no one seemed to think that was as important a fact as she did?

"Do you want me to talk to Mr. Bingley?" Jane asked.

"No!" Elizabeth sat up. "I do not want anyone to talk to anyone about this. It cannot be, so it will not be. Why can you not just leave it at that?"

Mary shook her head. "Should I ever love someone who does not notice me, which is an event that has a great chance of happening, I hope you do not give up as easily on helping me find happiness as you wish us to do for you."

"Do you love someone?" Elizabeth asked, hoping to turn the conversation away from herself.

Mary's eyes narrowed. "No, and I will thank you to not try to distract us from your happiness."

"Please," Elizabeth begged, "promise me that you will not push Mr. Darcy towards me. I do not want to marry a man who was forced to like me for I cannot see how that would lead to lasting felicity."

The room sat silent for what felt like an eternity to Elizabeth, though that was likely just due to her holding her breath as she waited for her sisters and Charlotte to promise they would not interfere.

"I know you are here for my happiness, Elizabeth. You have told me so. Therefore, while it might break my heart to promise you this, I will, simply because you have asked me to do so," Jane said just when Elizabeth was going to have to gasp for air because her lungs were crying out for it.

"I will not let you marry Mr. Ward if you love Mr. Darcy," Charlotte said. "Do you love him?"

Elizabeth rolled her eyes. "I admire him."

Charlotte scowled. "I think you more than admire him."

"Promise me that you will not push him at me," Elizabeth said.

"I promise."

"And Mary?" Elizabeth asked.

"I will not push him at you, but that does not mean I will not promote you to him if the chance arises." She shook her head as if thoroughly disgusted that she would have to promise even that much. "I love you." Her left eyebrow arched over an intense and disapproving gaze. "Why would I not want to try my best to see you happy? I do not see why you can put yourself through this party for Jane, but I cannot attempt to help Mr. Darcy fall in love with you."

"Please," Elizabeth begged. "Mr. Bingley already adored Jane. It is not the same."

"It is similar."

Oh! Stubborn was not a strong enough word for Mary at times.

"I promise not to push him at you," Mary said.

It would have to do.

"Mama wanted me to remind you that we are to go riding in half an hour," Jane said.

"Do we have to?" Elizabeth asked. "Can I not have a headache?"

"Do you want Mama to make a fuss?" Mary asked. "You know she will. She'll likely have someone like Mr. Ward gallantly riding off to fetch the apothecary because she will think it is romantic."

That was true. Their mother's favourite sorts of stories were the ones where a lady was rescued by a gentleman. And, to be honest, Elizabeth was not opposed to being rescued if there were a true need for it. However, a feigned headache was not the sort of calamity that required a hero to ride to her aid – especially, if that hero was not the one for whom her heart longed.

With a sigh, Elizabeth rose to change her clothes for riding. Maybe, while riding, she could find a way to love Mr. Ward and rid herself of the disappointment she knew would be hers if she allowed herself to continue to love Mr. Darcy.

Chapter 13

The day was bright and cool. It was a nearly perfect day for the first of October. Not only was the weather just as it should be, but the horses were fresh and eager to get exercise. Added to those facts, Miss Elizabeth was surrounded by her sisters, Miss Lucas, Bingley, and Mr. Ward, and she looked happy – or mostly so.

That was a good thing, was it not? He had suggested Mr. Ward to Miss Elizabeth, and it appeared as if his suggestion had been a good one. So, then why did Darcy's success feel like a failure?

"A fine lot of horses, is it not?' his cousin said as Darcy drew up beside him.

"It appears to be."

Bingley had enlisted the help of his neighbors to make certain that everyone at Netherfield, who wanted to ride, had a mount, and from all appearances, the neighbourhood had not disappointed in its provisions. If things continued to tick along as they were, Bingley's party would be remembered as a resounding success.

"Miss Elizabeth seems to have found her mark," Richard said.

Darcy glanced at his cousin and voiced what he thought was most likely the cause of his unshakeable sense of apprehension about Elizabeth and Mr. Ward. "Do you think they make a good match?"

Richard looked at Darcy in utter disbelief. "There is not a finer fellow for her here. Is that not what you told me?"

"That is what I thought." Now, he was not so certain. Miss Elizabeth did not look completely happy. She was mostly happy, but mostly was not good enough. Mr. Enfield would not have wanted for Miss Elizabeth to be only mostly happy.

"Then, what is the issue?"

"Her eyes."

"Her eyes?" Richard parroted as if he was uncertain if he had heard Darcy say what he had said.

Darcy nodded. "She smiles at Mr. Ward with her lips, but her eyes lack any sparkle."

"Miss Elizabeth's eyes sparkle?" Still, Richard seemed unable to understand what Darcy was saying.

"Yes. Normally."

"You have witnessed this phenomenon?"

"Yes." Darcy had spent a great deal of time admiring Miss Elizabeth's fine, expressive eyes. "She seems guarded. Even her features are not as animated as they have been when Georgie and I have met her in the garden." He would hate to be the person who had created a match that would not make Miss Elizabeth completely happy, and currently, she did not look anything like an entirely happy lady should look.

Before his cousin could formulate a response to what Darcy had just said, their solitary ride was interrupted by a most unwelcome intrusion.

"Mr. Darcy, you are a very fine rider," Miss Shaw said as she maneuvered her horse a little too close to his. She batted her lashes when she looked in his direction. She was one of Miss Bingley's most annoying friends. While Miss Bingley paraded her accomplishments in front of him, Miss Shaw was more forward and preferred coquettishness.

"Thank you." Darcy directed his horse to put some space between himself and Miss Shaw. "However, I am only tolerably good compared to my cousin."

"I could not see a great disparity between your skill and that of the colonel's. Could you, Caroline?"

Of course, Miss Bingley, though she was a few paces behind Darcy, would be with Miss Shaw. The two ladies were often inseparable when at soirees in town.

"The colonel is a fine rider, but I prefer Mr. Darcy's style."

"I would be surprised if you did not," Richard said. "It is a standard ploy. Do you not have any new tactics?"

The animosity between Richard and Miss Bingley had not lessened since that day in the drawing room when Miss Bingley had suggested that Lady Matlock was anything less than a paragon of goodwill.

"Tactics?" Miss Shaw cried before laughing in that cajoling fashion some ladies of the *ton* seemed to favour when they wanted to let one and all know that the person to whom they were speaking was not overly intelligent. "I am sure I do not know what you mean."

"Then you are as stupid as your friend."

"Richard," Darcy muttered.

"What?" Richard demanded in a sharp tone. "Miss Shaw knows precisely what I mean. Miss Bingley has used every ploy she knows to try to turn your head, Darcy. Flattering a gentleman's skill and saying that he exceeds all others in that particular skill is standard issue flirting. If I went into battle and used the same method of attack each time, only to be defeated over and over, I would either die in battle or be sent somewhere where my desperate lack of intelligence would only harm me and not the cause." He glared at Miss Bingley. "Let me inform you that nothing you have to offer or feign is what my cousin wants, nor do I wish to have you added to our family."

"Richard," Darcy grumbled.

"I do not like her."

"That is apparent," Miss Shaw shot back. "And I would dare to say that the feeling is mutual. However, Caroline is in possession of enough manners to not behave so reprehensibly as you are."

Richard chuckled. "She knows she will be sent packing if she does behave poorly. It is not because she is some meek, mild, and loving lady."

"Richard! Stop. Please." There really was no need to make this conversation with Miss Shaw and Miss Bingley any longer or more unpleasant than it already was going to be.

Richard gave a nod of his head, indicating to Darcy that he would do what he was asked – at least, for the time being.

"Have you found any gentlemen to your liking who are not my cousin?" he asked Miss Bingley. "I might be persuaded to help you snare them if you have."

Darcy fought not to roll his eyes. It was a better line of discourse, but only just.

"I would not tell you if I had," Miss Bingley answered very primly.

"Then, perhaps you should go look for one." Richard smiled.

Miss Bingley's eyes narrowed. "We came to discuss Miss Elizabeth with Mr. Darcy."

Now, she smiled, and Richard's eyes narrowed.

"Why?" he demanded.

"Because," Caroline replied with a lift of her chin, "Miss Elizabeth needs a husband, and Mr. Ward seems promising."

"Needs?" There was a growl of warning in Richard's tone.

"Yes, needs," Miss Shaw said. "I understand from Mrs. Hurst that if Mr. Bingley wants to buy Netherfield, and we would all like him to do that, then Miss Elizabeth needs a husband."

"Millicent!" Miss Bingley cried.

"I am only attempting to help a friend," Miss Shaw assured her. "Surely, the colonel and Mr. Darcy understand that your becoming the sister of a landed gentleman and, therefore, raising your position in society, is important to me because it is important to you in securing the proper sort of husband." Her eyes slid to Darcy.

"Some gentlemen do not care about such things," he said.

"Ah, but many do," Miss Shaw countered. "Why, my parents would not even let me consider Mr. Bingley, when he paid me some attention last season, and it was simply put down to the fact that he did not have an estate."

Bingley had paid particular attention to several ladies last season and all, including Miss Shaw, had been found wanting in some way. Whether or not Miss Shaw's parents would have allowed for a match between their daughter and Bingley was irrelevant. Bingley had not been tempted to even contemplate a match with his sister's friend. She had been a pretty companion when one was needed. Nothing more. Bingley was incapable of attending a ball and not dancing every set, and he was just the sort of gentleman who knew his duty in calling on those ladies after a soiree and escorting a few on drives as necessary. It was all part of the social game one played.

"Even with Netherfield, Bingley will still have come from trade," Darcy said.

"But he will have land," Miss Shaw countered, "and that is the important thing. One must always be moving forward to help expunge the taint of relations as far as one can."

"I have not decided to sell," Darcy said.

"Yes, you have," Miss Bingley argued. "That is why Charles is at Netherfield."

"That is how it began, but I find that the longer I am here, the fonder I grow of the place." And if he chose not to sell, then Miss Elizabeth would not have to marry until she had found a gentleman who could both make her smile and cause her eyes to sparkle. He glanced in her direction. She was still riding with her sisters and Mr. Ward.

"Do you grow fonder of the estate or its neighbours?" Miss Shaw's tone had turned catty.

"I see nothing wrong with the neighbours here compared to anywhere else," Darcy replied.

"Oh, I did not mean you found the neighbours to be less than enticing." She shared a speaking look with Caroline. "However, as I was saying many minutes ago, Miss Elizabeth seems fond of Mr. Ward. I would be happy to help promote the match, even if you choose not to sell Netherfield, for how could I not wish to see as many ladies as possible happily settled? And Mr. Ward would be a small step forward for Miss Elizabeth and her family."

"I do not delve in matchmaking," Darcy retorted. He had suggested some gentlemen to Miss Elizabeth, but that was all he was willing to do. Indeed, that might have been too much to have done. And he doubted very much that Miss Shaw was interested in anyone's happiness other than her own.

"If playing matchmaker for Miss Elizabeth is the only reason you came to speak to me, I am sorry to disappoint you. Now, if you will excuse me, I would like to let my horse run."

"Is there a reason you do not want her to make a match with Mr. Ward?" Miss Shaw asked.

Darcy ignored the question and patted his horse's neck. "Come on, boy," he said as he used his heels to urge his horse forward and away from Miss Shaw.

"A race!" someone shouted when Darcy galloped off with Richard following behind him.

"Dare you to catch him," someone else called.

Why must one galloping fellow on a horse mean a race? Darcy thought as the sound of hooves pounding the ground grew behind him.

"No, no, no!" a familiar female voice yelled. "I did not say to run."

Which lady was it? Darcy was certain it was not Elizabeth, for he would recognize her voice. He looked over his shoulder to discover who was in trouble and found that Miss Mary's horse had gotten caught up in the excitement of the other horses chasing after Darcy. She was holding her seat. That was good. And he could see her pulling back on her horse's reins, but the beast was not heeding the command.

"Richard," Darcy shouted and nodded his head back towards Miss Mary.

"Take the right," his cousin replied. "I have the left."

Darcy circled out to his right and turned back toward Mary only to discover that he was not alone in seeing to Mary's need for assistance.

"Pull back, Mary," Miss Elizabeth called to her sister as she chased after her.

"I am."

"Harder! Like you are taking your bonnet back from Lydia."

Miss Mary gave her reins a firm tug, and the animal shook its head but finally, began to slow.

"Keep pulling back," Miss Elizabeth said as she slowed her horse somewhat to match the pace of Miss Mary's.

"Well done, Miss Mary," Richard said as he reached the two Bennet ladies. "You, too, Miss Elizabeth."

The trio slowed to a stop next to Darcy.

"You ride well." Richard sounded impressed, as well he should be.

"Why were you racing?" Miss Mary demanded.

"We were not racing. Darcy wanted to gallop, and I did not want to be left with Miss Bingley and Miss Shaw."

Miss Mary opened her mouth only to close it again without saying a word. Then, she looked around until she spotted Miss Bingley and Miss Shaw. Her lips curled upward. "You abandoned them?"

"Yes."

She looked at Richard and, for the first time in all the times that Darcy had seen her in company with his Richard, she smiled. "Well done, Colonel."

Richard's head pulled back a bit, and he scowled as if confused. "Why well done?"

"I do not like them," Miss Mary replied. "They are horrid."

Richard chuckled. "I do believe we have found something upon which we agree."

"I am happy to hear you are not completely devoid of sense." And with those words, the Miss Mary, whom Darcy had become used to seeing make jabs at his cousin, returned.

"I will remind you that I rode to your rescue."

"And I thank you for doing so, Colonel."

"However, you do ride well," Richard added, "so I doubt you truly needed rescuing."

"Me? I ride well?" Miss Mary said in shock. "I thought you said that to Lizzy. She is a much better rider than I."

"It was meant for you both."

"Oh." Miss Mary seemed at a loss for what to say in response other than that one small word.

"Thank you, Colonel," Miss Elizabeth said, "and Mr. Darcy. I assume you were also riding to my sister's rescue?"

Darcy nodded. It was all he could do when she was smiling so brilliantly and her eyes were sparkling just as brightly. This was how she need to look at Mr. Ward if she was going to marry the man.

"I think we are all well now," she continued. "Shall we continue our ride, or do you wish to return to the house, Mary?"

Mary looked at her sister, then Darcy, and finally, Richard. "Will you and Mr. Darcy ride with us if we continue our ride?"

"Are you certain you do not wish to return to the house? We could see you back to the stables," Richard replied.

She looked torn between staying with those riding or returning to the house.

"We will ride with you no matter what you choose," Darcy offered. Riding a runaway horse would bring on fatigue as soon as her nerves settled. It would be best if she were to return to the house before that happened. "However, I will add, as a bit of persuasion, that Georgiana might like some company. She was disappointed to not be joining us for the ride."

Miss Elizabeth turned her horse towards Netherfield's stables. It seemed she was making the decision for her sister. It also meant she was not eager to return to Mr. Ward's company, a fact that both delighted and worried Darcy.

"Does your sister enjoy riding?" Miss Elizabeth asked.

"Very much so," Darcy answered.

"I do not get to do it as often as I wish." There was hint of regret in her tone.

"Mr. Enfield used to let Lizzy ride his horses. That is why she is a better rider," Miss Mary said. "She has had more practice. We have to share a horse at home."

"That is understandable," Darcy said. Not every household could afford to supply all the family with their own horses to ride. "Did Enfield ride with you?" he asked Miss Elizabeth.

She nodded. "Or when he did not, he would send Sam with me. He is a groom at Netherfield."

"Yes, I have seen his name in Enfield's journal."

"I think Sam liked Elizabeth at one time," Miss Mary said.

"He did not," Miss Elizabeth protested. "We were just good friends."

"Mr. Enfield seemed to think he admired you," Darcy said.

"He did?"

Darcy nodded.

"Sam married about a year ago," Miss Mary inserted as if it was important that Darcy knew that fact.

"I guess that means he got over his love for Miss Elizabeth," Richard said with a laugh.

"He did not love me," Miss Elizabeth protested.

"No, he *admired* you." The comment was said as if Miss Mary were taunting her sister about something.

"Admired is not the same as loved."

"I say it is."

"You would be wrong," Miss Elizabeth rejoined.

Darcy raised an eyebrow and looked at Richard. It seemed they had stumbled upon some unresolved argument.

"I would say the two words are nearly the same," Richard said.

"Nearly the same is not the same."

Richard laughed. "No, but I do see how someone might hold to the idea that they are. Tell me, Miss Elizabeth, what do you say makes them different?"

Miss Elizabeth tipped her head and studied Richard, giving Darcy a moment to appreciate the way her neck turned.

"Admiration fades more quickly and less painfully," she said.

"That is a good answer," Richard said.

Darcy had to agree.

"I can admire someone or something," she continued, "without needing to be admired by that person or thing in return. I might like to be admired in return, but if I were not, I would imagine that the disappointment is not as crushing as if I were to love someone and not have that love returned." Her eyes flicked to Darcy for a moment before returning to his cousin.

"That is also a good answer," Richard said. "Unrequited love is a great sorrow – not that I know from personal experience – I am just surmising based on what I have read and heard."

"Oh, of course," Miss Elizabeth assured him. "That is what I am doing as well."

Miss Mary made a soft noise of disbelief that earned her a glare from her sister.

Was Miss Elizabeth in love with someone who did not love her in return? Darcy looked over his shoulder to the group of riders who were becoming smaller and smaller on the horizon. Mr. Ward seemed to be smitten with Miss Elizabeth. Surely, she knew he was, and if she did know of his admiration…

"Do you fear Mr. Ward does not love you but only admires you?"

Miss Mary chuckled at Darcy's question while Miss Elizabeth looked at him as if she wanted to be anywhere but there, with him, discussing Mr. Ward.

"No."

"Then, you know he loves you?"

Again, Miss Mary chuckled.

Miss Elizabeth's jaw clenched before she once again said, "no."

"You do not love him?"

Miss Elizabeth shook her head.

"But you admire him?"

"I do not see why you need to know that," Miss Elizabeth said.

"I think that is a no," Richard said.

"I am just trying to understand why you are always with him if you do not love him or even admire him," Darcy replied honestly. "There were two other gentlemen on the list I gave you. What about Mr. Harrison or Mr. Morris? Do you admire either of them?"

Miss Elizabeth glared at Miss Mary who was once again chuckling. "No," she said. "Neither Mr. Harrison nor Mr. Morris seems to be interested in me."

"They are fools not to be," Darcy muttered.

"Thank you." She gave him a sad smile.

Was she truly sad that neither of those gentlemen showed her any preference or was it something more?

"If you must know," she continued, "I am attempting to love Mr. Ward, but so far, I have not succeeded. Do not misunderstand me, he is a wonderful man. It should be easy to love him, especially since he does seem to admire me."

"But you cannot?" Darcy fought to keep himself from smiling at that news.

"Not yet."

"Do you believe it is possible?" Darcy's heart clenched at the thought of her succeeding in loving Mr. Ward. What was the matter with him? He was not the sort of gentleman who was ecstatic one moment and in the depths of despair the next.

"I do not know, but I must try. Now, could we talk about something – anything – other than my need to marry?"

Her lovely eyes begged him to grant her wish. How could he refuse? Those eyes needed to sparkle. He needed them to sparkle so that he could know she was happy and well.

"Is this the horse Mr. Enfield always let you ride?" he asked.

Gratitude shone in her eyes when she told him that this was indeed the horse she always rode. That soft, pleased shining was just as lovely an expression as a joyful twinkling.

Thankfully, Richard picked up the conversation about horses and carried it away as he waxed eloquent on his passion for all things equine, for it gave Darcy time to ponder who Miss Elizabeth loved and why it made him so delightfully happy that it was not Mr. Ward.

Chapter 14

OCTOBER 4, 1811

"My aunt said you did very well at archery," Georgiana said as she strolled arm in arm with Elizabeth two days after the horseback riding excursion.

"I did not do as well as Mary did, but I did manage to surprise myself with my success. I think I have your brother to thank for that." To Elizabeth, the best part of the whole exercise had been hearing Mr. Darcy compliment her shots.

"Was Mr. Ward duly impressed?"

Inwardly, Elizabeth sighed, but she did not let her smile falter. "He was."

Mr. Ward grew more and more attentive each day, and Elizabeth was beginning to worry that he might actually present her with an offer before the house party ended. She was not ready to accept him. Not yet, and maybe not ever. But this parcel of land on which she and Miss Darcy walked could not be sold if she did not find a way to will her heart into accepting him, since no other gentleman seemed to show as much interest in her as Mr. Ward did. Oh, there had been several who had sought her out the past three days, but none seemed as smitten as Mr. Ward.

"My aunt speaks about Mr. Ward and you a great deal when we are closed up together with Fitzwilliam and Richard at night before we all retire to bed," Georgiana said.

"Does she?" That was surprising. "What does Lady Matlock say?"

"Only that she has noticed a deepening of the gentleman's regard for you. However..." Miss Darcy cast a wary look at Elizabeth.

"However, what? Do not leave me in suspense."

"However, she does not seem to think the admiration is returned, or, at least, she does not think it is returned in equal measure."

"It is not," Elizabeth admitted. "I wish it were, but it is not."

"Why do you wish for it so badly?" Georgiana asked. "You are still young. Surely, there is time for you to find a gentleman whom you can admire as greatly as he admires you."

The true issue was that Elizabeth had found a gentleman to admire greatly, but he did not seem to admire her as anything other than a friend. And then there was her sister Jane who had found a gentleman to admire and who loved her in return. This estate was important to that gentleman's future, and, therefore, her sister's happiness by extension.

"This garden needs to be sold." Elizabeth pulled her new friend toward their bench.

"But it does not have to be sold right away. Fitzwilliam has told me he is not settled on selling Netherfield."

Not selling Netherfield? "When did he tell you that?" Elizabeth plopped down on the bench far less gracefully than she had expected to do.

"The night before last."

Were all her efforts to participate in this party for naught? "What will Mr. Bingley do?"

Miss Darcy shook her head. "I do not know, but I suppose he will purchase a different estate."

"But then, he will not be near Jane." And if there was no promise between them before Mr. Bingley left, what would become of Jane's heart?

"He will find a way to be near her," Miss Darcy assured Elizabeth. "I have never seen him so in love with anyone. Even Fitzwilliam says it, and he is not one to catch on to things pertaining to love as quickly as some are." Her eyes searched Elizabeth's as if she was looking for something in particular.

"My mother says that gentlemen are often half in love before they even know they have begun."

"I do not know about all gentlemen, but that does seem to be accurate where my brother is concerned. I dare say he will be utterly smitten and have lost his chance before he realizes he is in love with a lady."

"No, surely not!"

"I assure you that it is true."

"But your brother is so clever. Even Mr. Enfield mentions how quickly Mr. Darcy catches on to things."

Miss Darcy shook her head. "Not when it comes to females and matters of the heart, although, I will say, he seems to agree with my aunt that you are not happy with Mr. Ward as a future husband, which is a strange thing to be certain. He has known you for such a short time, and yet, he seems to understand you to some degree."

"We have spoken together about Mr. Ward and my need to marry. You have been there for some of that."

"No, it is more than that. I am not sure I can explain it. There is this heightened awareness of everything you do and an attempt to understand it. I assure you that he is not so with everyone." She turned toward Elizabeth. "He says it is because he had learned so much about you in Mr. Enfield's journals, and I would have to agree that that is a large part of it. I do not think you and I would be such ready friends if it were not for the wonderful things that I have learned about your character from what Fitzwilliam reads to me. I mean, I think we would have progressed to this level of friendship with time, but the journals have hastened the acquaintance."

"I dare say I would have to agree. I have learned so much about your brother through reading Mr. Enfield's thoughts," she looked out toward the wildwood and smiled sadly.

According to Mr. Enfield, there was no gentlemen of finer character in all of England. That her former neighbour and friend thought well of Mr. Darcy was not hidden, and Elizabeth's opinion of Mr. Darcy echoed Mr. Enfield's. How was she supposed to find a husband when her heart belonged to the incomparable new owner of Netherfield?

"Last night, I read a passage that told a story about your brother." Elizabeth turned to share what she had read with Miss Darcy, but decided to only say, "I will let you read it later," when she saw Miss Shaw and Mr. Evans approaching.

It was likely to be another introduction to a possible husband because, for two days now, Miss Shaw had been doing her best to make sure each and every gentleman in attendance was provided with a few minutes of Elizabeth's time. While Elizabeth found it annoying, her mother had expressed her delight over Miss Shaw's actions last night by saying, *"Perhaps it will provoke Mr. Ward, or some other gentleman, to act quickly so that he does not lose you."*

Elizabeth did not want anyone to act quickly. She was not the last piece of exquisite lace in a showcase, which some lady would buy on impulse, only to realize later that her purchase was not the correct thing for her project. Elizabeth had no desire to be discarded when the exhilaration of the chase was over.

"Miss Elizabeth," Miss Shaw said as she stepped into Elizabeth's Garden, "I was just telling Mr. Evans about how Mr. Enfield left you this parcel of land, and he wished for an introduction."

"We have met," Elizabeth said. "Yesterday, Mr. Evans was kind enough to retrieve my arrows for me." He had seemed pleasant enough, but he had not appeared to show any interest beyond making sure that the order of play could move along at a steady pace. It made Elizabeth worry about what Miss Shaw had told him to pique his interest.

"But, yesterday, you were not able to take a walk together," Miss Shaw said with a flutter of lashes. "We mustn't deny Mr. Evans that pleasure, even if it seems as if that is what Mr. Ward would like us to do."

She leaned toward Elizabeth and lowered her voice. "Mr. Ward did not look happy when Mr. Evans asked to walk with you when I mentioned the idea. Therefore, I believe, Mr. Evans really does need a chance to walk with you before you are no longer available for garden strolls with anyone but Mr. Ward."

"Ward does seem to favour you quite highly," Mr. Evans agreed.

And yet, he was willing to interfere between her and Mr. Ward. That did not speak very highly of Mr. Evans' character in her mind. If she had wanted to walk with him before she would not now. However, she had not wanted to walk with him at all, so now that apathetic desire had turned more toward revulsion.

"As you can see, I was having a private discussion with a dear friend." Elizabeth motioned to Georgiana.

"That is not what house parties are for, my dear," Miss Shaw scolded her sweetly. Too sweetly.

Who was she to tell Elizabeth what she could or could not do? "I believe they are, at least, in part, designed for that purpose."

"Some might say they are if a lady's goal is to snare the brother of her dear friend." Again, Miss Shaw fluttered her lashes. It was a most annoying expression.

"I do not plan to *snare* anyone," Elizabeth retorted.

Miss Shaw simply smiled in return. It was a patronizing smile. This woman, Elizabeth decided, was as dreadful as Mrs. Hurst and Miss Bingley combined.

"Mr. Evans has an estate in Surrey and a house in Mayfair, and his income is twice that of Mr. Ward. Surely, you can see how it would be a very poor thing to not at least consider him before settling on Mr. Ward."

Elizabeth's eyes grew wide as she looked from Miss Shaw to Mr. Evans. Did he not care that he was being presented as a peddler might put forward his wares to a lady in the street?

"Do not be missish, Miss Elizabeth," Mr. Evans said with a laugh. "I am under no illusion that this gathering in the country is to fraternize without purpose. I am in want of a wife, for I am not getting any younger, and I would like to enjoy my children while I am still spry enough to do so."

How old was he? He did not have any gray hairs. He did not wear spectacles. He was not as thin as some. There was a pudginess to his waistline, and he had a few lines that showed near his eyes when he smiled. However, he certainly did not look as if his dotage was only years away.

"A father should be able to dance a reel as well as his son does in his first season, I say, but that will not happen if I do not marry at an appropriate age and beget a son shortly after."

Oh, my! Elizabeth glanced at Miss Darcy. Begetting children was not an appropriate conversation to be having with her present – not that Elizabeth deemed it appropriate to be having without Georgiana present either.

"And I understand there is also some urgency to your finding a husband quickly," Mr. Evans continued, causing Elizabeth to gasp. He seemed not to notice, or if he did notice, he did not care that he had affronted her. Instead, he looked around the small garden they were in. "My coffers are not wanting, but the money from the sale of this garden would not be unwelcome." He turned his eyes back to her. "I could provide a good life for you." He held out his hand. "Come. We will discuss what I can provide while we walk."

"Whom else have you told?" Elizabeth demanded of Miss Shaw.

"What do you mean?" she asked with another annoying flutter of lashes.

"Do not play coy with me." Anger and humiliation warred to gain the upper hand in Elizabeth's mind. "Besides Mr. Evans, whom have you told about this garden and my supposed need to sell it?"

"I have told no one." Again, her irritating lashes fluttered.

"Then, how does Mr. Evans know what he knows?"

"That is quite simple, my love," Mr. Evans said. "Mrs. Hurst told me, just as she told several others."

Mrs. Hurst! Of course, it had been Mrs. Hurst. The unscrupulous prattler! Elizabeth drew a breath through her nose and exhaled slowly. "I am sorry to disappoint you, Mr. Evans, but neither I nor my garden are for sale." She turned to Miss Darcy. "Allow me to see you back to the house."

Georgiana wrapped her arm around Elizabeth's.

"And Miss Shaw, please refrain from arranging any further meetings with gentlemen for me. I find I am not in the market for a husband just yet."

Miss Shaw smirked. "That is not what your mother says."

Elizabeth dipped a curtsey. "Good day."

"Are you well?" Miss Darcy asked when they were several steps away from Miss Shaw and Mr. Evans.

"No," Elizabeth answered honestly. "It might be best if I quit the party. Mama and Mary can see to it that Jane and Mr. Bingley continue to grow fond of one another."

She blinked against the tears of mortification that wanted to fall. All the attention she had been given by gentlemen who had not given her more than a second glance began to make sense. "Do you think Mrs. Hurst was tempting the gentlemen who sought me out yesterday with the promise of a greater dowry than I have, due to that garden?" she whispered.

"I do not know, but it might be true." Miss Darcy gripped Elizabeth's arm more firmly.

"Mama will not be pleased with me for refusing to walk with Mr. Evans or for having spoken so sharply."

"I am," Miss Darcy replied. "I am certain I could not be as brave as you."

"I was not brave. I was angry – I am angry."

"Even so, I am still happy you did what you did."

"I appreciate your support. You are a dear friend. However, I am not sure that what I did was the right thing to do, for now, the tale of my snub of Mr. Evans will circulate with great embellishments, which will, no doubt, paint me as a shrew."

"My aunt will neither believe it nor tolerate it."

Georgiana was loyal, much like her brother was, according to Mr. Enfield.

"I trust you are correct, but it matters not. Once a story is told, it is very hard to retract it." And the story would be told far and wide quite quickly if Miss Shaw were as scheming as Elizabeth thought she was. Even a season in town might find the story harming her chances there. "The damage has been done. It would be best if I were to just go home."

"Oh, please stay. I will miss you dreadfully if you go. I am to return to town with my aunt at the end of the party."

"I will also miss you, but I cannot see another way to answer this. If I am not here, then maybe the story will lose some of its interest." Elizabeth stopped at the edge of Netherfield's garden and turned to look back. "I wish I could just give that garden away. If I could, I would give it to your brother and be done with it. Then, there would nothing for these gentlemen to seek at the cost of my heart." She laughed bitterly. "Who would have thought that I would have to deal with fortune hunters, such as they are? I never would have imagined it. How much can that small section of garden be worth?" Truly, it could not be worth overly much.

"I do not know about the price of a garden, but I do know about fortune hunters. There was one who nearly succeeded with me." Miss Darcy's cheek glowed rosy. "I am not supposed to talk about it, but please know that I understand somewhat of what you feel."

Elizabeth's breath caught in her chest. This sweet young girl had been preyed upon by a gentleman like Mr. Evans? She was not even out yet!

"My fortune hunter was more charming than Mr. Evans, however," Georgiana continued. "He pretended to love me and only me. He never once mentioned my fortune until my brother intervened and put an end to things."

"Mr. Franklin's dog, who would rather bite you than his supper, is more charming than Mr. Evans."

Miss Darcy giggled. "Oh, Elizabeth!"

"And you are very fortunate to have such a good brother." The best brother. The best gentleman. That is who Mr. Darcy was. It was dreadfully disappointing that he was not one of the gentlemen on her list, for she could so easily love him. Indeed, she knew she already did.

She pushed the idea of Mr. Darcy returning her affections out of her head. She was feeling melancholy enough about Mr. Evans, Miss Shaw, and Mrs. Hurst. She did not need to add another, heavier layer to her mood. If she had a pound for each time she had pushed Mr. Darcy out of her mind –

She stopped walking just in front of the door to Netherfield. There was something in that thought. If she had a pound... if she only had a pound... A smile tipped her lips. That was the answer to her current problem.

"Are you well?" Georgiana looked at Elizabeth with concern.

Elizabeth nodded and smiled. "Yes, yes, I believe I am for I have had a wonderful idea."

"What is it?"

Elizabeth followed her friend into the house.

"I cannot say," she said as they climbed Netherfield's grand staircase. "I am not even sure it is possible, but I will know soon." Just as soon as she could speak to her uncle.

Chapter 15

Darcy straightened his sleeves and gave his waistcoat a tug before stepping into the drawing room where everyone was gathering before dinner. His eyes scanned the room for the lady he hoped to make his wife. A revised list of one name was neatly folded and tucked in his pocket.

He had wrestled with himself for a day and a half about why he was so pleased that Elizabeth did not love Mr. Ward and had concluded that it was because somewhere along the way, he had fallen in love with her. And not just a little in love with her. She had crept into his heart and overtaken it completely. He could not bear the thought of Mr. Ward or any other gentleman ever taking her from him without his making an attempt to secure her first. Therefore, he hoped to give her the new list as soon as possible and discover his fate.

"I have not seen her," his aunt whispered as she came to greet him. "Her sisters and mother are here, but she is not."

He and his aunt had discussed his plans, and Aunt Ada was nearly as happy with his decision as he was. There was no way for anyone to be quite as happy with the idea of Elizabeth as Mrs. Darcy as he was.

"Do you have any idea where she might be?"

Aunt Ada shook her head. "Mrs. Bennet said she was either with Georgiana or possibly Mr. Ward since that gentleman had asked to speak to Miss Elizabeth privately."

Darcy's heart plummeted to his stomach. Ward was going to offer for Miss Elizabeth? Was he too late to prevent it?

His aunt held out her hand to him, and he took it. "Go see if she is with Georgie before you think the worst," she said as she gave his hand a squeeze.

Darcy spun on his heels and took the stairs two at a time in his rush to get to Georgiana's room. Reaching her door, he knocked urgently.

"Bingley will not be pleased when he has to repair a door due to your pounding," Richard said as he came down the hall.

"Have you seen Elizabeth?" Darcy asked him just as the door to his sister's room opened.

"Why are you looking for her?" Georgiana asked.

"I need to talk to her before she decides to marry Mr. Ward." He ran a hand through his hair. He might already be too late if she was not with Georgiana. "Is she with you?"

"No."

He closed his eyes and expelled a breath. He was too late.

"Are you well?" Georgiana asked him.

He shook his head. Richard grasped Darcy by the shoulders. "What is wrong?"

"I love her."

"Yes, I know. However, I am surprised you have figured it out already," Richard replied.

"You love her?" Georgiana clapped her hands in delight. "Oh, I had hoped you would."

"What does it matter now?" Darcy grumbled. "And what do you mean you knew?" he asked Richard.

"The only fellow who notices that a lady's eyes sparkle is the one who is in love with her," he replied.

Darcy blew out a breath. "Well, since Mr. Ward has asked to speak to her privately, and she is not with Georgiana, I believe it is up to him now to make her eyes sparkle." The words tasted as bitter as they were painful to utter. "I am going for a ride. Tell Lady Matlock that I will eat in my room later." If he could force himself to eat at all.

Both Georgiana and Richard said something to try to stop him, but he was not listening to anything but the splintering of his heart. He was too late. Elizabeth was lost to him.

"Fitzwilliam!" Georgiana ran down the hall after him. "She went home."

He stopped and slowly turned toward her. "Elizabeth went home?"

His sister nodded. "She said it was the only way to keep the gossip from being too entertaining."

He shook his head. "Gossip? What gossip?"

"Yes, what gossip?" Richard had joined them.

"Elizabeth discovered from Mr. Evans that Mrs. Hurst has told several gentlemen that Elizabeth needs to marry to sell her garden to you before you can sell Netherfield."

"Why that despicable —" Richard halted both his movement toward the stairs and his grumble when Georgiana grabbed his arm.

"Elizabeth told Mr. Evans that neither she nor her garden are for sale."

Darcy had to smile at that. If he truly still had a hope to make her his wife, she would never have to sell it.

"She was so brave." His sister's face shone with admiration. "Though she said it was not bravery, just anger."

"And that is why she has gone home?" Darcy asked.

"She was certain that by dinner time, she would be painted as the worst sort of shrew."

"But what about Mr. Ward? Aunt Ada said he asked to speak to her privately."

Georgiana shook her head. "I do not know. Is he in the drawing room with the others?"

"He was not there when I went in search of Elizabeth." Of course, he could have just been late. Or, he could have found Elizabeth before she left for home.

"Allow me to check." Richard did not wait to be given permission. He just immediately galloped down the stairs.

Georgiana and Darcy followed him at a more sedate pace but not slowly. There was hope, Darcy told himself with each step he took. Elizabeth might not be lost to him.

"Elizabeth is not with you?" Mrs. Bennet met Georgiana at the bottom of the stairs. Behind her was Richard, Lady Matlock, and Mr. Ward.

Darcy breathed a sigh of relief. Ward was alone. "She is not with you?" he asked the man.

Mr. Ward shook his head.

"You did not speak with her?" Darcy asked.

"He has not," Mrs. Bennet answered. "But he was going to."

"It was not as you were expecting, madame," Mr. Ward said. "I was going to withdraw my suit."

"Withdraw your suit?" Mrs. Bennet's hand flew to her heart. "Why ever would you do that?"

"I do not believe I am capable of engaging your daughter's heart." He looked at Darcy. "Unfortunately, I think it is engaged elsewhere." He gave a bow of his head as if acknowledging a loss to an opponent.

A smile that started deep within Darcy's soul spread across his face. He had not lost her. He had only to find her and persuade her to consider him.

"Georgiana said she went home," he said as he moved toward the door. "I will ride to Longbourn and discover the truth." Both about her whereabouts and her heart.

A footman scurried from his post outside the drawing room to open the door for Darcy, but before either he or Darcy could reach the door, it opened.

"Elizabeth," the name rushed from Darcy's lips on a breath. She was here. He moved towards her and offered her his hand.

She gave him a questioning look but placed her hand in his.

"Georgie said you had gone home."

"I did, and then I went to visit my uncle."

"Why would you go to see him?" Mrs. Bennet asked.

"To see to the arrangements for the disposal of my inheritance."

Darcy's heart was unsure if it should continue beating as it always had or if it should drop to his stomach again or return to the breaking it had been doing before.

"Have you..." He drew a shallow breath since drawing a deep one was impossible at the moment. "Have you accepted an offer of marriage?" He drew another shallow breath as he tightened his grip on her hand as if that could keep her from being snatched from him. "Please, say you have not," he whispered.

Her brow furrowed.

"I have not."

"I do not understand," Mrs. Bennet said. "You cannot dispose of your inheritance until you are married."

Elizabeth pulled her hand free from Darcy's grasp and moved toward her mother. "I was seeing to the *arrangements* for it. I will not be sought after by gentlemen hoping to scheme their way into Mr. Darcy's or Mr. Bingley's pockets." She looked past her mother.

It was then that Darcy realized the others from the drawing room had spilled into the entrance hall.

"When the time comes for me to sell my garden, *I* will be the one to negotiate the settlement, and the portion of the proceeds that will go to my husband shall be no more nor any less than one pound."

"One pound?" her mother cried. "How will that ever help you find a husband?"

Elizabeth shifted her gaze back to her mother and smiled softly at her. "If the man I choose to marry cares so little for me and my family, then I have made a very poor choice in accepting him."

Mrs. Bennet's look of confusion mirrored Darcy's thoughts. What was she talking about?

"As Uncle Phillips has written it, at my request, whatever remains after the pound has been given to my husband is to be split equally between you, my sisters, and me. How could I keep such a wonderful gift as the one Mr. Enfield gave me without sharing it with those whom I love most dearly?"

Elizabeth looked from her mother towards those gathered near the drawing room door. "I wanted to make certain that whoever marries me does so because he loves who I am and not what I possess. A person's value is not found in pounds and pence, nor is it measured by acre, field, or flowerbed."

She was perfect. Utterly, absolutely, without a doubt, perfect. Darcy could feel the love he held for her growing with every beat of his heart. She was the very one for whom he had always been searching, for she was a lady who would love him for himself and not Pemberley, the treasures in his coffers, or his connections. And such a lady was precisely whom he want at his side to help guide his sister.

"Good luck, I say."

Lady Matlock turned to Mrs. Hurst. "Why do you say that?"

"Who is going to marry her without the inducement of her garden?"

"I will."

The assembled group gasped like one large, many-headed beast at Darcy's declaration.

"If she will have me," Darcy added.

"She would be a fool not to," Mrs. Bennet said as she gave Elizabeth a little shove towards Darcy.

"Perhaps we should all return to the drawing room so that Mr. Darcy and Miss Elizabeth can speak privately," Aunt Ada said.

Darcy heard some shuffling of feet, but his eyes did not move from looking at the lady he loved. "I made a new list." He drew the folded paper from his pocket. "As you will see, I have included the same qualifications as before, but I have added two more."

He waited as she unfolded the list that only bore his name. Once she had it open, he began speaking again. "I would like to think that I have a good heart and a kind disposition. However, you can verify that with my sister if you wish. That aside, I know I have a healthy fortune, not that you care about its size."

Her cheeks were flushed, but her eyes sparkled as she smiled at him. She was the loveliest of all women. She truly was, for he could see her heart shining in her eyes and no one had a heart that was more beautiful than his Elizabeth's.

"Those three items are important," he continued, "but they pale in comparison to the next two requirements. As you can see, I have put a tick mark under only one of those columns for I know that I love you most ardently. The final column I have left for you to fill in since only you can determine if my love is returned in equal measure." He took a step towards her. "That last item should have always been the only question to consider. I would not want you to be tied to anyone, not even me, if you cannot love him with your whole heart." He took her hand. "Can you love me?"

Her eyes scanned the paper she held once more. "Were you going to give me this list tonight?"

He nodded. "I was looking for you to give it to you before dinner. When I heard that Mr. Ward had asked to speak to you in private, I…" he blew out a breath and dropped his gaze to their joined hands. "I thought I had lost you. I cannot describe the agony that immediately sprang to my mind and heart."

"You love me?"

"Yes, and I will love you with my dying breath."

She lifted his hand to her lips.

Her kiss was soft and sweet. It was also a promising sign, was it not? A lady would not kiss a gentleman's knuckles if she were going to refuse him, would she?

"And my garden?" she asked.

"It will be yours forever, though the price of it shall be negotiated in the marriage papers and dispersed of as you said."

"Does that mean you are not selling Netherfield?"

"That is what it means." He released her hand so he could cup her cheek with his right hand. "As I thought about it and you last night when I should have been sleeping, I think that Netherfield would make a grand inheritance for one of our children, that is if you will marry me. Please say you will marry me."

He wrapped his left arm around her and drew her close. "Be Georgiana's sister. Be the mother of my children. Be my helper, my dearest friend, and my beloved until we are parted by death, and each of us, in our time, joins Mr. Enfield in heaven."

Tears filled her eyes, and he caressed her cheek with the pad of his thumb.

"I have longed for you to be on that list you gave me since the day you gave it to me," she said as a tear slid down her cheek, only to be brushed away by Darcy's fingers.

"You are handsome," she continued, "and you have made my heart flutter simply by being near. However, you are so much more than that. Your character cannot be surpassed. I know it both because Mr. Enfield wrote such lovely things about you and because I have seen it in your actions. You cared about me even when you did not know me. You considered what I would desire in a husband when you created your list, and you were the only one who did not tell me I needed to marry and sell my garden, even though you were the one who had the most to gain from its sale."

"No," he said with a shake of his head, "I had the most to lose by your marrying and selling your garden. I did not know that when we first met, but I know it now. The prize was never your garden nor was it Netherfield or the sum of money I would part with to buy that parcel of land from you. The treasure is you, my love. It has always been you and always will be you. Mr. Enfield knew that. It is clearly spelled out in his journals. I can see it on almost every page now that I have realized that you, my dearest love, are what he wished to leave me. Marry me?"

"I would be foolish not to," she answered with a smile. "For I love you most profoundly."

He brushed his thumb across her cheek again. His gaze lowered to her mouth. "Will you kiss me?"

"Everyday, forever."

Lowering his head, he pressed his lips to hers and knew in an instant that he had never before been more right than he had been when he said that she was his treasure, for the taste of her was more intoxicating than the finest wine in Netherfield's cellar – and Enfield had been a lover of fine and expensive wines. The feel of her in his arms as he drew her as close as could be done was more delicious than any cake Netherfield's cook could produce – and Darcy had sampled many excellent cakes when visiting Enfield. Her whispered *I love you,* when he paused in kissing her to allow that sentiment to bubble out of him as it insisted it must do, was more precious than anything the world could offer now or in the future. And their coming together because of a pretty piece of Netherfield's garden was, without question, the absolute greatest and best inheritance that had ever been bequeathed with quill and ink.

If you enjoyed this book, be sure to let others know by leaving a review.

~*~*~

Want to know when other books in this series will be available?
You can always know what's new with my books by subscribing to my mailing list.

leeniebrown.com/subscribe

(There will, of course, be a thank you gift for joining because I think my readers are awesome!)

[Do you enjoy stories where an inheritance and a scheming relation play a role in the happiness of the hero and heroine? Then, allow me to recommend Not an Heiress and share an excerpt from the first chapter with you.]

Chapter 1

Mary Bennet tucked the book she had just finished reading back on the shelf and pulled out another. The selection of books at Rosings was not small, but -- she sighed, there were just not enough books of substance, at least, not the substance she sought. She flipped through the pages covered in verse.

There was only so much poetry she could read, and she was certain she had surpassed her limit. In her opinion, poetry did nothing to secure the mind in the realities of propriety. In fact, lately, it had done the exact opposite. It had her dreaming of walks in the forest and along streams with her hand in that of a very handsome gentleman -- a gentleman who was not within her reach.

She shoved the book back onto the shelf. Poetry was not what she needed. He would be here soon. She needed to have something more serious to read. Something that would keep her mind from wandering to his wide shoulders and muscular calves. Young ladies should not have such thoughts, especially young ladies who were determined to be an example of propriety to one and all. However, no matter how she tried, Colonel Richard Fitzwilliam could not be thought of as serenely as other men. It was really quite vexing how he tormented her with thoughts that caused her to smile at impropriety. A sermon was needed and the sooner, the better.

"If Lady Catherine is looking for me, I will be at the parsonage," Mary told Fletcher, Rosings' butler, as she tied on her bonnet in preparation for her walk. "I will not be long."

"The parsonage?" Lady Catherine de Bourgh stood in the doorway to her sitting room just down the hall from where Mary was attempting her escape. "We have guests arriving. It would not do for you to be gone when they arrive, and if I know my nephews, they will be early just to vex me."

"I will not be long," Mary tried to keep the pleading tone from her voice. "I only wish to borrow a book from my cousin."

Lady Catherine's eyebrows rose. "Are there not enough books in the library?" She knew precisely the sort of book Mary sought, but it was better to not let the young lady know.

"It is lacking in sermons." Mary looked at Lady Catherine's toes. Lady Catherine was not pleased to have her library or any part of her home criticized, nor was she particularly fond of Mary's choice of reading material. Mary had endured more than one lecture on broadening her repertoire.

"It is lacking in nothing that a young woman should need." Lady Catherine had taken a liking to Mary when she met the young lady at Pemberley the second summer after Lady Catherine's nephew Fitzwilliam Darcy and Mary's sister Elizabeth had married.

Mary was the most likely of the three youngest Bennet sisters, who were in residence that summer, to need improvement and need it the earliest. Lydia and Kitty did not seem to lack an interest in society the way Mary did, nor were Lydia or Kitty in as great a need of a husband since they were younger than Mary.

However, there was something else that endeared the young lady to Lady Catherine -- nothing that could be quantified beyond a spirit of gentleness mingled with a will of iron. She smiled. It would be lovely to have such a lady added to her collection of relatives in a closer fashion. It had not escaped her notice how often she found the young lady watching Richard nor how often Richard found reason to be in the presence of Mary.

Mary's shoulders drooped. "I have faithfully read the novels you gave me and the book of poems. May I not read just one book of sermons?"

Lady Catherine pursed her lips. "One book?"

Mary nodded.

Lady Catherine sighed. "Very well, but be quick."

Mary dipped a curtsey. "I will, my lady."

Lady Catherine watched her scurry out the door. It might be best if Mary were gone when the others arrived. It would make discussing her with Darcy and Elizabeth a good deal easier.

"Have the tea things brought in in half an hour," she said to Fletcher before returning to her sitting room. She sighed. The house was so empty these days without Anne and Mrs. Jenkinson to keep her company. It was partially why she had requested of Mr. Bennet that Mary come to stay with her.

She chuckled. Her meeting with the gentleman had been very productive. Not only had she gotten permission for Mary to come to stay at Rosings, but she had also received his blessing to play at matchmaking for the one whom he considered his least-likely-to-marry daughter.

She settled into a chair that stood in just the right place to see the drive and took up her stitching. She would not be caught unawares. Her nephews might attempt to ruffle her feathers by thwarting her carefully scheduled life, but they would not succeed. The thought of ruining their fun with a bit of her own pleased her excessively. She would know when her guests had arrived well before they had stepped one foot from their carriage.

She did not have to wait very long. The tea service was just being laid out when she spotted them. Darcy's fine carriage appeared first, and then Richard followed, seated high on his horse.

He was a fine specimen of a gentleman. Even she could see that. For all the detractors that found him less handsome than his cousin -- which he was since there were few as handsome as Darcy -- there was an equal number who found him enticing, especially when he was riding his horse or causing a general stir with some fascinating tale. Mary would be a very fortunate young lady to have such a husband.

And he would do well to have a sensible and devoted wife. Lady Catherine gave a little shrug. It was perhaps Richard who was getting the better end of the bargain. Mary was no wallflower, no matter how much she might attempt to be one. True, she did not shine like Jane or sparkle like Elizabeth, but she was not without charm. It was just that hers was the kind of beauty that lay quietly, waiting to be noticed.

Lady Catherine laid aside her stitching and watched as the carriage came to a stop and Richard jumped down to claim Alexander from his parents. He would make an excellent father despite his tendencies to exuberance and impropriety. She could not help smiling as he trotted off toward the garden with a laughing child on his shoulder.

It appeared the moment had come, and she smoothed her skirts nervously as she rose to greet Darcy and Elizabeth. With neither of the objects of her scheming present, now would be the best time to inform her other guests of her intentions to see Mary and Richard happily wed.

Acknowledgements

There are many who have had a part in the creation of this story. Some have read and commented on it. Some have proofread for grammatical errors and plot holes. Others have not even read the story and a few, I know, will never read it. However, their encouragement and belief in my ability, as well as their patience when I became cranky or when supper was late or the groceries ran low, was invaluable.

First and foremost, I want to thank God for giving me the passion, ability, and opportunity to write. Then, I would also like to say *thank you* to Zoe, Rose, Kristine, Ben, and Kyle, as well as my Patreon patrons, who followed this story as it developed and waited, as patiently as one might do, from one Friday to the next, to read a new chapter. I feel blessed through your help, support, and understanding.

And finally, I want to thank my husband for, without his somewhat pushy insistence that I start sharing my writing, none of my writing goals and dreams would have been met. I love you dearly.

More Books by Leenie

You can find all of Leenie's books at this link

bit.ly/LeenieBBooks

where you can explore the collections below

~*~

Dash of Darcy and Companions Collection

Marrying Elizabeth Series

Sweet Possibilities and Sweet Extras

Willow Hall Romances

The Choices Series

Darcy Family Holidays

Darcy and... An Austen-Inspired Collection

Teatime Tales (Sweet Austen-inspired Novelettes)

Other Pens

Touches of Austen

Nature's Fury and Delights (Sweet Regency Novelettes)

About the Author

Leenie Brown has always been a girl with an active imagination, which, while growing up, was both an asset, providing many hours of fun as she played out stories, and a liability, when her older sister and aunt would tell her frightening tales. At one time, they had her convinced Dracula lived in the trunk at the end of the bed she slept in when visiting her grandparents!

Although it has been years since she cowered in her bed in her grandparents' basement, she still has an imagination which occasionally runs away with her, and she feeds it now as she did then — by reading!

Her heroes, when growing up, were authors, and the worlds they painted with words were (and still are) her favourite playgrounds! Now, as an adult, she spends much of her time in the Regency world, playing with the characters from her favourite Jane Austen novels and those of her own creation.

When she is not traipsing down a trail in an attempt to keep up with her imagination, Leenie resides in the beautiful province of Nova Scotia with her two sons and her very own Mr. Brown (a wonderful mix of all the best of Darcy, Bingley, and Edmund with a healthy dose of the teasing Mr. Tilney and just a dash of the scolding Mr. Knightley).

Connect with Leenie

Subscribe to Leenie's Mailing List:

leeniebrown.com/subscribe

Website:

leeniebrown.com

Patreon:

patreon.com/LeenieBrown

Facebook:

facebook.com/LeenieBrownAuthor

MeWe:

mewe.com/p/leeniebrown1

Instagram:

@leenie.b (Leenie B Books)

E-mail: *LeenieBrownAuthor@gmail.com*